# Footsteps in
# the Blood

# Footsteps in the Blood

## Jennie Melville

St. Martin's Press
New York

Library of Congress Cataloging-in-Publication Data

Melville, Jennie.
    Footsteps in the blood : a Charmian Daniels mystery / Jennie Melville.
        p.    cm.
    "A Thomas Dunne book"
    ISBN 0-312-09813-8
    1. Daniels, Charmian (Fictitious character)—Fiction.
    2. Policewomen—England—Fiction.    I. Title.
    PR6063.E44F66    1993
    823′.914-dc20                                                          93-24387
                                                                                   CIP

First published in Great Britain by Macmillan London Limited.

First U.S. Edition: November 1993
10  9  8  7  6  5  4  3  2  1

M
MEL

# Footsteps in
# the Blood

## PRELUDE

After the hottest summer for years, it was a wet autumn. Rain falling like tears on the brown leaves in the Great Park of Windsor.

Charmian Daniels called it the worst autumn of her life. She was a highly successful policewoman who had had a lot of publicity together with great success. She thought some, if not all, the terrible things that happened that autumn were due to the very fact of her success. She had attracted attention, and that was dangerous.

As soon as a woman is successful, puts her head above the parapet, she comes under fire.

It had happened to other women, she could names names.

Now it was her turn. Hers, and that of two other young and successful women.

The first victim in the terrible happenings was a woman, too. Well, a girl still, and not much of a success. She deserved better than a death, though. She deserved time.

Charmian thought she could place the very moment when it all started to happen.

It was the day after her biggest triumph to date. Or at least, the most publicised, involving, as it did, a touch of royalty. The day she had been photographed wearing an Anne Klein skirt with a Katherine Hammett shirt and a Marks & Spencer blazer. A drugs case, a porn-ring case involving children, a sickening beast of a case where she had helped trap most of the guilty men, if not all.

It was a good photograph.

Admit it, she said to herself, I looked better than I usually do, photographed better than I should have done. I'd actually had my hair cut and kept my lipstick in place. I was in luck, and I suppose that was maddening.

To the wrong person, literally so.

The photograph showed the outer woman: a confident, strong woman who took the eye. Of course, inside her was the usual bag of doubts and insecurities but these did not show.

The photograph was important as a spur to action on the part of someone, Charmian was right about that.

However, there was one other episode that was crucial that she knew nothing about.

Early on that autumn, packing to come home after a bruisingly hard spell of work across the Atlantic, she had paused for a glance in the mirror of her hotel room.

She looked at herself. If I didn't know it was impossible at my age, I would say I'd grown about an inch.

But it wasn't that she'd grown, she had just lost weight. You shouldn't lose weight like that, should you? Was it dangerous, a bad sign?

What a thought to come home with.

# CHAPTER ONE

## Thursday, October 5

It was the worst-attended funeral of the year. And in a town which prided itself on its good turnout at funerals. Windsor liked a funeral, royal if possible, but others would do.

Just two young women and a huddle of policemen. The huddle was because of the rain. One of those soft, pervasive autumnal rains which get everywhere. No day to be buried.

The two young women stood side by side as the coffin was lowered into the grave. One was wearing a sensible brown tweed suit which, in a fit of unsuitable frivolity, she had teamed with a blue satin blouse. The other young woman was dressed in black suede: skirt, jacket and a kind of cloak, all of which looked exceedingly expensive and not particularly funereal. They were the only mourners except for the professionals: those from the funeral parlour and from the police. One of the girls, she in the tweeds, was a police detective herself, and understood exactly why the police were there and whom they were watching. Her. And her friend.

One, or both, of them might be in danger; she knew that too.

'I hate funerals,' the tall girl in brown tweed was on the point of saying aloud, when she was checked by the sound of earth falling on the coffin. 'Especially when it might have been my own.' She kept this thought inside her too, giving a brief look at her companion.

The person they were burying had been a young woman too.

A wet windy October day in the royal riverside town of

Windsor with the sovereign's standard fluttering over the castle and the river gleaming like dark silver.

The churchyard was in the old part of the town, beyond the complex of shops in Peascod Street and Sheet Street. St Saviour's Church was a red-brick Victorian structure, somewhat Italianate in style and with its churchyard well filled with ornate memorials. The present corpse was lucky to find a bit of spare land, but it was in a less favoured, scrubby stretch of ground beyond which the railway ran. Not a smart area. But she hadn't been a smart girl. Not socially or intellectually.

It was the quietest of funerals. Certainly the press would have been there in great numbers if the time and place of the interment had not been kept secret, for the girl who was buried had died with brutal violence.

The two young mourners deposited their flowers on the newly turned earth and then moved away. White violets from one, she was rich, and white carnations from the other, who was not rich and did not like carnations but it was all the florist had that morning.

'I hate funerals.' This time it was said aloud.

Dolly Barstow was Sergeant Barstow of the local CID and the officers on the other side of the grave were known to her. They recognised her, could be said to be watching her but weren't saying anything. Dolly felt she had aged ten years in the last two weeks.

'We owe her this. Coming here today,' answered Kate Cooper, she who had donated the white violets and who did her mourning in a black suede suit from Ungaro. 'We killed her.' Kate did not look at Dolly but stared straight ahead.

A pause. Dolly was not accepting that. 'No, by God, we didn't.' She took Kate by the arm. 'Come on, let's get out of here. We've done our bit.'

Kate let herself be led off. Dolly was right in a way, but if they had listened . . . only listened . . .

'We did listen,' said Dolly.

'Not properly, we didn't take what she said seriously.'

'I don't know about that,' said Dolly. She had felt very serious.

'It was us she threatened and demanded money from. First me and then you. Said there was a man after us, and if we paid her, she'd tell us who. We laughed. First you, then me.'

'Not quite laughed,' said Dolly.

'And then she ended up getting shot on our doorstep. Of course I feel guilty.'

'I shouldn't say that too loudly.'

'You mean one of your colleagues will arrest me?'

The two of them lived above each other in small apartments in a block with a distant view of the castle and in sight of the river. The girl they had just buried had died in front of that apartment block in Merrywick, a smart residential area between Eton and Windsor. Spilling out her guts on the small patch of grass between them and the road.

'There was Charmian. We could have told her. I've always been able to tell her everything. Or nearly everything. We ought to have told her.'

'She knows now.'

Charmian Daniels, Chief Superintendent in the Metropolitan Police in London, head of a special unit, was Kate Cooper's godmother. Kate had always been able to call on her in times of trouble. In many ways, Kate was closer to Charmian than to her own parents. Annie Cooper was a well-known artist, and Jack – what was Jack? He had been hobbled, his daughter thought, by having neither the talent nor the inherited money of his wife.

'I don't like the way they are looking at us.'

Dolly rather agreed with Kate there, but she thought it was Kate they were looking at. Any person who gets too close to a violent death is liable to earn such scrutiny, and the lovely Kate was well worth looking at.

One of the police officers strolled over.

'Miss Cooper? I'd like to talk to you if I may.'

Kate felt her throat go tight; she swallowed. 'Here?'

'At your home, if I may.' He was a tall young man, Sergeant Bister, known by name to Dolly Barstow, but not someone she had worked with. Naturally, she thought, it would have to be an officer who had had no contact with me. An aggressive, ambitious young man if reports were true.

'I have answered a lot of questions already.' To her horror Kate found herself being defensive. 'I don't think I know anything I haven't told you.'

11

Dolly took a step nearer Kate, lining herself up by her friend. Bister looked at her. Keep out of this, Barstow, his eyes said, or your turn will come. If you hadn't been out of the town when Nella Fisher got hers, you'd have had the treatment already. You may yet.

'All the same, Miss Cooper, there are some other questions to be asked.'

Kate felt all the air go out of her lungs as if a great hand had squeezed her. 'All right, when?'

'At your convenience.'

Kate did not answer. What was convenient? Never.

'Now, then, this very hour,' he said briskly. 'Get it over with. Always better. I'll drive you.'

Kate looked across at her low black Saab. 'We came in my car.'

'Sergeant Barstow can drive that for you.'

Kate made an irresolute half-turn: 'Dolly?'

'Yes, I'll follow you, Kate.'

Kate handed her car keys over. 'Watch it,' she said to Dolly in a hollow voice. 'Power steering.' She got into his car beside Sergeant Bister. It was unmistakably a police car, with another officer inside as well.

I think I'm going to be arrested, she thought. It can't be happening to me. It's a nightmare.

Her own private nightmare.

She sat huddled next to him, while he drove her speedily to Number 33A, Didcot Square, Merrywick. Dolly Barstow lived above in 33B.

Dolly followed close behind them, not letting them out of her sight. There were some nasty elements in this case, as she was well aware. Police corruption being one of them.

The cars stopped, one behind the other. They had arrived in the neat prosperity of Didcot Square. Two small blocks of flats surrounded by grass and gardens.

Where the whole dirty nightmare had started.

There was a car parked at the kerb. A small but powerful-looking car with one woman sitting at the wheel. With relief, Kate recognised both car and passenger. She saw Sergeant Bister give it a startled look.

12

As the two cars drew up, Charmian Daniels got out, and advanced towards them, ignoring Bister and concentrating on Kate and Dolly. She did not look pleased.

'You're a hopeless pair,' she said. 'Trying to handle this on your own. Why didn't you call for help?'

# CHAPTER TWO

## A backward look at Thursday, September 7, and then a return to the day of the funeral

Merrywick, situated on the edge of Eton, with its face directed firmly towards the royal town of Windsor and its back resolutely turned on the industrial belt of Slough, called itself a village.

Merrywick had a church, a school, a post office and a village green. It also had a smart hairdresser who did beauty treatments, several boutiques selling expensive clothes, and an antique shop. There was a small employment agency which doubled as a delivery and messages service. You could go in there and fax documents out, or you could get them delivered by hand by a messenger boy on a bicycle as in olden days. This last service, although fashionable and much used by the *nouveaux riches* of the district, was distinctly the most expensive, as was to be expected. Merrywick was a thoroughly modern village.

A half-dozen Victorian cottages, where farm labourers on the nearby Merry Farm had formerly worked, lined up in a neat terrace along one side of the village green. Each cottage was now a valuable property, hiding in its carefully reconstructed interior a modern kitchen and several bathrooms, while outside was a carefully paved and planted garden with, possibly, a conservatory of Victorian design. The cottages were charming but would have surprised their original inhabitants. There was one old-time resident whose run-down home and unpainted front door had for some time been a subject of criticism and even hostility from the newcomers, but feelings had swung in her favour lately. Mrs Beadle was now cherished as a genuine relic, proof that Merrywick was a real village.

Behind the green lay crescents and squares of newish, large houses which looked as prosperous as they were. And beyond these lay a cluster of houses in their own grounds. The owners of these houses were rich, and on their way to being even richer. When that happened they moved away to Gloucestershire or Wiltshire, to 'real country', and bought a 'place' which was called The Manor House, or The Old Rectory, although there was no requirement that the manor should ever have had a lord or the rectory an incumbent.

The owners of these large Merrywick houses never shopped in the boutiques for clothes, or had their hair done in the village; they were, indeed, rarely seen locally, but their big cars – the Rollses and the Porsches – swishing through were a much appreciated local sight. It indicated that Merrywick had quality.

Tucked away at the back of all these glories, but suitably near the church, was the undertaker's office with his chapel. This did good business because death was a fairly frequent visitor to Merrywick. It was a tough, competitive world these prosperous householders lived in and the casualties were not few. In fact, their average expectation of life was about the same as the farm labourers and artisans whom they had dispossessed.

If you drove out of the Merrywick in one direction you soon came to Eton, a village dominated by one institution and that one a school: the King's College of our Lady of Eton Beside Windsor, founded by that most devout of English kings, Henry VI. If you drove on further yet, then you came to the very town of Windsor about which all else clustered, with its castle, home farms and parks. The royal castle was a town in itself containing communities of clerics serving the great Chapel of St George, units of soldiers on guard duty, and the delightful houses of the Poor Knights of Windsor, a charity founded by Henry VIII, and now reserved for distinguished retired officers. And at the centre of all, the Court, which comes and goes as fashion and the season demand: always there at Ascot and Christmas, never there when the grouse fly in Scotland.

15

Industrial and commercial Slough had the most convenient railway station and the best buses, but Merrywick usually chose to travel via Windsor. A better address.

Why didn't we talk to Charmian? Kate asked herself as she walked up the path behind her godmother. Because she wasn't here for one thing. In New York attending a police conference on inner-city crime.

Why didn't I telephone Charmian? thought Dolly Barstow as she parked her car. I knew where she was. I could have made contact. But I was too proud. Didn't want help. Wanted to manage on my own. There was another reason too, of course, but for the moment, her mind circled that darker thought and did not dwell on it.

Too late now to ask for help in a dignified way for either Kate or herself. Better leave it. She wasn't sure if she herself was in danger either of physical attack or arrest, but she felt pretty sure that Kate was.

The procession went up the garden path. First Kate Cooper with Charmian Daniels – Chief Superintendent Charmian Daniels – then the two local CID officers, and finally Dolly Barstow herself – Sergeant Dolly Barstow – also of the local CID.

Behind them was the patch of grass on which the girl they had just buried had died.

Up the stairs to the front door of Kate's apartment. Inside to her small but beautiful sitting room. Its beauty was sparse and bare, Kate was into minimalism, but she had inherited her mother's good taste and got it right.

They all trailed in. The two policemen were wetter from the rain than anyone else and as no one asked them to take off their coats they did so unasked and dumped them in the hall.

Charmian turned round.

'I want to talk to Miss Cooper. May I have a minute, Sergeant Bister?' She had his name pat, he noted sourly. Had done her homework before she got here. Trust her. With her rank and friends, all things were made easy. Or easier, he told himself, not meaning to make it absolutely pain-free if he could help it. 'You can sit in if you like.'

The sergeant thought about it, considered Charmian's rank, her friends and her influence, then said yes.

'Come on then,' said Charmian to the two young women. 'Tell me what happened.'

Four weeks ago, in early September, although it seemed longer, the girl, who called herself Nella Fisher, but was later discovered to be called something quite different – in fact, to have several names, layers of names, you might say, each possibly with a different personality, but for the purposes of this case was Nella Fisher for ever, rang the bell of Kate Cooper's flat.

'Kate?'

'Yes, I'm Kate Cooper.' Kate did not know the girl, so she held the door cautiously, only half-open, not inviting the girl inside. She had met some strange characters in her somewhat adventurous life, and this might be one of them. The girl had long fair hair which was falling across her face so that she had to keep brushing it away. A narrow, pale face with dark-brown eyes. The colour of the eyes, so dark, did not match the paleness of her skin and hair, as if she had somehow managed to bleach all colour out of them, leaving only her eyes untouched. She was wearing tight jeans and a baggy shirt. It had been raining, it was the wettest autumn on record, everyone was going around rained on, but this girl looked damp and bedraggled beyond anyone.

Like a little lost cat that can't get in from the rain, thought Kate.

With a rush of compassion that surprised her, she said: 'You'd better come inside.'

And the girl was in, silently, without another word. Just like that little cat that didn't wait for a second asking.

She offered her name: 'Nella Fisher.' Her voice was quiet, the vowels and consonants carefully shaped, as if her natural speech might have been quite other.

This slight falseness came across to Kate Cooper, who frowned.

She doesn't look dangerous, thought Kate. I'm certainly bigger and stronger than she is. Just why do I feel apprehensive then? Distantly, she seemed to hear her godmother warning: Kate, what did I tell you? Look before you leap. 'What is it you want?'

'You. I want to talk. Something I want to tell you.' She was looking around her. 'This your place?'

'Yes.'

Kate had painted the deep-yellow walls herself and, stippling and marbling being no longer fashionable, had invented a kind of wavy, dragged effect that gave an added dimension to the walls so that the corners seemed to melt into an apricot distance. It made a good background for the black *chaise-longue* from Milan. So far, except for three big black leather pillows on the floor and a tall green plant on a marble stand, this was all the room contained.

'It's pretty good.'

'Most people think it's weird.'

'They don't know, do they?' The girl took one small step into the room, not venturing too far. 'Besides, you'll be adding to it.'

'Probably not.' Kate was cool. 'So what is it?'

'I don't know how to put this, but here goes: I think you're in trouble, and I can help.'

Kate absorbed the information silently. 'What sort of trouble?'

'A man. He'll rush you if he can. Jump on you.'

'You mean he'll rape me?'

'Not sure exactly what he's planning. Or how he'll do it. I'm not sure what he's planning.'

She was repeating herself too much, thought the sceptical Kate. She didn't look drunk or high on anything, but she certainly seemed to be on a fantasy kick. That was how Kate saw it.

'Has he got in touch with you? Had any messages, any telephone calls?'

'Certainly not.'

The little cat face took on a thoughtful look. 'Not even sure it's you he's after. It might be that other one. The police one.'

'Dolly Barstow?' The name was bounced out of Kate's lips in her surprise.

'Is that her name? Yes, her then.'

'If I believe you – and I'm not inclined to – tell me, who is this man?'

18

'I'm not quite sure if I can tell you that yet. But I'm working on it. Might take some money.'

'Ah.' Kate thought they were getting somewhere. 'I don't buy goods at the door. You'd better go to the police. Tell them what's worrying you. They're better at sorting that sort of thing out.'

If there was anything in it, which she doubted.

'The police?' The girl laughed. 'They'll be the last people to go to.' She strode to the door. 'OK, so you won't listen. More fool you, you might regret it, but I'll be back. You can pay me then.'

After she had gone, closing the door quietly behind her, Kate went to the window to watch her leave.

But like all little lost cats she had disappeared into the undergrowth and was not to be seen.

She had to have gone somewhere. There was a belt of trees and shrubs surrounding the block of flats and she must have gone into those.

Unless she had gone to Dolly Barstow.

Dolly answered the telephone at once, which was so like her, she never wasted a minute. 'Yes? I'm washing my hair, so be quick. I'm dripping all over the carpet.' Dolly took her hair and her possessions seriously. Not having been born rich like Kate, she knew they had to be paid for and might not easily be replaced.

'You might be going to be called on by a lunatic. If your doorbell rings, ignore it.'

'What are you talking about? Who is the lunatic?'

'A girl, calls herself Nella Fisher. I thought she was like a little lost cat looking for a home. The name mean anything to you?'

'No, nothing.' But she did not have the names of all the local lunatics on her personal computer, and there were always new lunatics coming in. 'What does she want?'

'Money, I think,' said Kate thoughtfully.

'And what's her message?'

'That I am in danger from a man. Or it might be you.'

Next day, September 8, when Dolly came home from work, she found the girl, sitting, her back to the wall, by her front

19

door. The same jeans, the same shirt but with a sweater slung round her shoulders. Today was dry but cold.

Dolly stared at her, trying to get her measure. 'Yes?' she said carefully. 'What do you want?' Not a lost cat, she thought, more like a little cat that has been out hunting and caught something but is not sure how welcome home it is with its prey. A nervous cat?

'To talk to you.' The same gambit as with Kate, Dolly noticed. 'I'm Nella Fisher.' She stood up, thin and under-nourished-looking, her fair hair straggling unbrushed down her back, but she had put some lipstick on and her hands were clean. 'To warn you. There's someone after you. A man. You are his obsession. I'm almost sure it is you.'

Dolly did not open her door and ask her inside. She'd be in like a flash, Dolly judged, and maybe hard to get out again. Although I could pick her up and carry her, she thought.

Instead she laughed. The girl didn't like being laughed at. Cats don't.

'Don't laugh.'

'Nella, this is good advice I am giving you: go away and don't come back. You leave me alone and I'll leave you alone.'

The girl took a step away. 'That's a threat.'

Dolly shrugged.

'You police are all alike. Well, watch yourself, that's all I can say.'

The next day she was back again. This time sitting in Kate's car, left unlocked as usual.

'You'll do. You're the one with money.'

'And that was it?' Charmian asked.

'Then,' said Kate. 'I didn't give her any money.'

She came back again on September 11, Kate explained, and told the tale that she worked part-time in a pub, where she had heard two men talking. They had talked of a third man, a man obsessed with a woman. From what they said, she had identified the woman as either Kate or Dolly.

Nella said she knew the men by sight, and needed money so that she could drink where they drank and follow them about and identify the man that was dangerous. She would not consider going to the police; she said they would be worse than useless. Kate said she hadn't believed all this, but hadn't known what to make of it, except that the girl seemed desperate for money.

So that was the story and now it was a wet October and she was dead.

Dolly and Charmian looked at Sergeant Bister sitting quietly in the corner, taking it all in. 'So what did you think it meant?' asked Charmian.

'You tell me,' said Kate. 'Nothing probably. I thought she was a liar. A fantasist. People do make up tales, get to believe them. The silly thing is, I was getting to like her. She called on you for sympathy and somehow I couldn't help showing it. She knew it, too.'

Dolly said: 'I didn't like the police innuendo, but it probably meant nothing. I agree with Kate that the girl was a liar.' Out of the corner of her eye she saw Sergeant Bister relax his shoulders a little. 'I didn't like her, by the way. She was never going to win me over, but with me I don't think she was trying. She said I was going to be the victim, but Kate was the one with the money.'

'I would never have given her any,' said Kate. 'Anyway, then it all happened.'

The girl had come back the next day, and the day after, and every day for almost a fortnight. On the last occasion Kate, returning home, had found her busy at her own front door.

'I thought she was trying to get in. Pick the lock or something. I thought she had a knife. She had something sharp in her hand.'

Sergeant Bister got up and went to the window to look out, as if disassociating himself from what was being said inside this room.

Of course, he knows it all anyway, Kate thought. I've told the tale to him already. He's heard it all.

Kate liked his style. Tom Bister was an attractive man, but they were not meeting as she would have chosen.

She went on with her tale. 'She shouted at me. I thought she was going to attack me and I gave her a push. She fell down the stairs, still shouting, and then she ran away.'

There had been witnesses. The postman delivering a parcel to a flat on the floor above, a florist with a bunch of flowers.

The postman had testified that Kate had shouted she would kill the girl if she came back. She had a gun and would shoot her.

'Did you say that, Kate?'

'I might have done.' Kate had a temper and had been known to show violence. 'And she had cut my hand. I was bleeding. I was very angry.'

'Had you been drinking, Kate?'

'No, certainly not.'

'Drugs?'

'No.' Kate was vehement. This did not mean that Charmian believed her any more readily, but it meant she accepted the statement for what it was worth at the moment. Private questioning could come later, when Sergeant Bister was out of the way.

'So Nella went away?'

'Yes, I saw she wasn't really hurt by the fall and I thought that was the end of it.'

Only it was not.

Next morning, September 18, Nella Fisher had been found on the lawn in front of the flats, shot dead.

Her blood and brains oozing out on to the grass.

'Did you have a gun, Kate?'

In his corner, Sergeant Bister stirred in his self-imposed silence.

'I did have one. I bought it in India last year.'

'What for?'

'I was frightened of snakes.'

'Do you have a licence?'

'No.' Kate looked unhappy. 'Didn't seem important.'

Charmian made an irritated noise. 'What sort of gun, was it?' Sergeant Bister looked interested.

Kate sounded flustered. She stumbled her words. 'I don't know . . . I didn't really look.'

On that next morning the girl had been seen by a local resident out walking his dog. She had been found just a minute before which was his bad luck because otherwise he would never have seen her, she was hidden by the bushes.

'I always wondered what happened to her when she was away

22

from here,' said Kate. 'What she was like when she was on her own. Where she went.'

'Don't you know?' asked Charmian quite savagely. 'She went home. Home was one room on the outskirts of Slough industrial estate. Not a prime residential area. She had a bed, and a table and sink, no bath, no lavatory, they were down the hall. She had photographs of you two stuck up on the wall.'

Kate looked surprised.

'Also one of me.'

A rare, vivid shot of Chief Superintendent Charmian Daniels looking well dressed.

In the silence, Sergeant Bister stood up. My turn now, his stance said silently. He didn't need to speak.

Kate said in a voice which she was controlling but could not prevent sounding nervous: 'I'll do this on my own, please, Charmian.'

'Kate,' began Dolly.

'You too, Dolly. There's coffee in the kitchen.'

In the kitchen, Dolly said: 'All this may not be what it seems.'

'Go on. Coffee with milk or without?' Charmian listened as she poured the coffee.

'I wasn't quite straight in there when I said I didn't accept the police innuendo, and that she was a liar. She may have been, but I think she did know something.'

'You'd better explain yourself, Dolly.' Charmian felt that tight feeling at the pit of the stomach that told her she wasn't going to like what was coming.

Dolly wandered round the kitchen, cup in hand. She too was nervous. 'I hope this kitchen isn't bugged.'

'Come on, now.'

'Joke.' She drank some coffee. 'Well, here it is. For some time now, and for various good reasons, I have thought that we have a bad apple in the barrel here.'

'Are you talking about police corruption?'

Dolly nodded, without saying any more.

Charmian said in the most unfriendly tone that Dolly had ever heard from her: 'And these various good reasons?'

Dolly said: 'Can we go into that later? All I want to say

23

now is that I think I may be the only person with direct, seen-with-my-own-eyes evidence.'

Charmian studied her face, checking it for conviction, for sincerity. She liked Dolly, trusted her, but this was dangerous talk.

'You mean you saw something or someone?'

'With my own eyes.'

'So you have a name?'

For the first time, Dolly hesitated. 'I think so.' She flushed a little. 'I could explain all this better later. Not here.'

She nodded towards the next room, indicating Sergeant Bister.

'And you think this Nella girl knew? And that was what she wanted paying for?'

'Yes. I was the one threatened. She more-or-less told Kate the victim was probably me. A policewoman, she said that. And I have been prowling around certain quarters, I may have been noticed. Probably was. I have felt threatened.'

'Even before she spoke to you and Kate?'

'Yes.' Dolly nodded. 'But I thought I was imagining it.'

'And you think she was killed because she knew something and was going to tell you? To shut her mouth?'

Dolly shrugged. 'Why not?'

Charmian put her coffee cup down. It didn't taste so good now, as if Kate had made it that morning and let it stand, slowly gathering heat and bitterness.

From the window she could see the rain hitting the trees, making the leaves bend downward.

'I wonder why she wanted paying?' she speculated. 'Did she look mercenary to you?'

'Look? Who knows about looks? She looked a loser. Yes, I think she did need some money. I thought she might be on drugs. Have a habit that needed keeping up, but the pathologists say no, she was clean.'

'What did you make of the girl?'

Dolly considered. 'She'd been around. She had a kind of used-up look. But I sensed ambition.' She shook her head. 'Or a strong emotion of some sort. Something was powering her.'

Charmian turned back from the window. 'Damn Kate for having a gun.'

Dolly gave a half-smile. 'That's Kate.'

'You can't blame her, she's been spoiled. Look at her parents. I admire her mother, and respect her work, but her father must have been difficult to grow up with.'

Annie and Jack had had a difficult marriage. On and off, sometimes quarrelling, sometimes together. Annie had always had more money than Jack.

'You know he made a pass at me at a party?' Dolly said.

'What did you do?'

'Laughed. He hated it.'

Charmian poured some more coffee and went back to the subject in hand. She had slapped Jack's face once herself. Of course, Annie did not know. Or did she?

'All the same, Kate's gun cannot have been used to shoot the girl.'

'Of course not,' said Dolly.

'As soon as it's examined that will show up.'

'The sooner the better in that case. Neither of us enjoys being under suspicion of murder.'

'It can't be anything to do with you,' said Charmian.

'You'd be surprised how it rubs off.'

Charmian drank the coffee and listened for sounds from the next room. She could hear Sergeant Bister's deeper tones, but could not make out what he was saying, and once or twice she thought she heard Kate laugh.

Laughter seemed unlikely in the circumstances, but that seemed to be what she heard. Yes, there it was again, a low rumble from Bister and a short laugh from Kate.

Dolly could hear it too and didn't seem to like it. Kate was just sure enough of herself and her attractions to think she could get away with things with Tom Bister.

Charmian didn't like the laughter either and she frowned. Sometimes you didn't know where you were with Kate.

But the Kate she loved couldn't have shot that girl, whatever the provocation. In the past Kate had been capable of showing violent anger, but she had matured and grown wiser. Her character had seemed to become as lovely and graceful as her looks.

No, it was impossible to think of the mirthful, vibrant girl who had shared her house in Maid of Honour Row for a season as a killer.

Besides, it didn't ring true. What possible motive could there be for deliberate murder? The story as she'd been told it by Kate and Dolly provided no reason for Kate attacking the girl, other than in self-defence.

Unless Kate wasn't telling all she knew.

'Any idea what lines Bister and Father are thinking along?' Charmian asked Dolly.

Charmian knew Chief Inspector Father, they had worked on a case together in the recent past. She had a wary respect for him, she did not always like his style, but he got results.

'They haven't said, and I'm supposed to be on leave although I hang around, but my guess is that they think the girl was on the prowl, met Kate late one night and got into a quarrel with her. Somehow, as a result of that, she got shot.'

'Kate wouldn't have a gun on her.'

'That's probably what's worrying them.'

'It must make them accept that the killer was someone outside, not Kate.'

'I think they have the idea that there's a lot more to it than they know.'

So there is, thought Charmian. There has to be.

'Is Fred Elman on the case?' She didn't trust Inspector Elman not to go for the quick answer.

Dolly shook her head. 'On a course in Birmingham. He'll be back.' She kept all feeling out of her voice. Elman was a good boss to her in his way and she didn't want to put him down.

Also, she was in a very delicate situation herself, half a suspect and half imagining herself the victim.

'Have you said anything about your own suspicions to any of them?'

Dolly looked thoughtful. 'I sort of mapped out a hypothetical case to Father over a drink and he didn't like it at all. Wouldn't wear it. Mind you, he'd had a few. Not sure if he remembers now.' And she wasn't sure if she wanted him to remember either. It might have been a mistake to talk at all. She needed a confessor quite outside the magic circle. Even Charmian wasn't quite neutral, you could pick it up in her voice.

Dolly sat hunched over her mug of coffee. The bright red mug had been made by Kate's mother; a noted potter and artist, the mug belonged to her so-called 'Red Period', one of her best. Kate's kitchen was red too, what there was of it, Kate not having done much to the room except paint it. The red reflected a sort of pinkiness on to Dolly's cheeks so that she looked flushed. She was a pretty young woman, more muscular than she appeared, and highly attractive.

Dolly and Kate had been good friends for several years now, but they were different in character and ambition. This was reflected in the clothes they wore: Kate's were always more expensive and more flamboyant than Dolly's conservative outfits. The different styles were carried through into their homes: Dolly's was practical, comfortable and even cosy; Kate's had great zest – you might not sit at ease, but you noticed where you were.

But both young women were united in their respect and affection for Charmian Daniels; she was Kate's godmother with a good record of loving help and support over the years, while for Dolly she was a role model whose distinguished career Dolly meant to follow. She had been a pathfinder in her time, had Charmian. There was an added complication at the moment for Dolly knew that a career problem loomed for Charmian who was being offered a new position of great trust. She desperately did not want to harm the upward movement of a woman she admired: this case might just do it. For herself, too, it represented a threat.

She thought Charmian looked tired, as well-groomed as ever, but thin. Thinner than she remembered.

For a moment both women sat in silence. Charmian broke the silence.

'Where is George Rewley these days?' Sergeant Rewley was an intelligent, subtle and sensitive young detective whom Kate had seemed to like a lot. 'I haven't seen him around lately.'

'I don't know. I think something went wrong between them, but I don't know what. The trouble with Rewley is that he's almost too perceptive, he probably saw a lot that other men would not notice, and he'd speak, because he doesn't hide things, and you know Kate. She does bristle at criticism. You have to handle her.'

'I would have thought Rewley could.'

'But you have to want to,' said Dolly shrewdly. 'Rewley might not have wanted a relationship you have to handle like a bomb. Not all men do.' Especially police officers who had a lot of that sort of work in their professional lives and liked a bit of peace at home. And Rewley, too, was in many ways a rather special person.

Charmian considered. She knew her difficult Kate, who seemed to work through men like washing her hands. A pity. Rewley could have been a help just now.

'It's a pity she has a gun at all,' she said aloud.

'As long as it's the wrong gun,' said Dolly.

Charmian gave her a sharp look. It had to be the wrong gun.

'I tell you I don't feel confident of anything at all,' said Dolly, responding to the look.

The voices in the next room stopped. For a perceptible moment there was dead silence.

'Good or bad?' asked Dolly. Then she answered herself. 'Beats me.'

The door opened and Kate and Sergeant Bister came into the kitchen. Kate did not have the air of a girl who had just gone through a searching interview. She looked composed, having regained any self-confidence she might have lost in that earlier brush with Charmian. She met Charmian's eyes with what her godmother called her 'matter-of-fact' look. That was a good sign.

Sergeant Bister's expression was harder to read. Perhaps he was pleased with himself. That was a less good sign.

Charmian was thoughtful. From what she had heard of Bister he knew where he was going and was not likely to have been misdirected even by the lovely Kate. That easy confidence of Kate's, product of money and social class, could be self-delusive.

Kate said: 'I think the sergeant might like a cup of coffee. Pour one for me too, Charmian, please. I've just got to go and get something.'

'Three guesses what it is,' murmured Dolly under her breath.

Sergeant Bister heard but ignored her. 'Kate and I have gone over the night when the girl was killed, and the other episodes. I think I've got a clear picture.'

'I wish I'd been here,' said Dolly. 'I might have heard or seen something.'

'But you were in London?' Just as well, Barstow, he thought to himself, or you'd be in more trouble than you are.

'Yes. As you know.'

'Having dinner in London at the Stafford Hotel? Nice place.'

'It was a family dinner party,' said Dolly, 'to meet my mother's new husband.'

Her third, isn't it? thought Bister, who had checked. Out of interest really, because he did not think it added anything relevant to the case, but he always checked everything. In any case, it told him a bit more about Dolly Barstow in whom he was interested. Professionally and privately interested.

He took his cup of coffee. Black but with three lumps of sugar.

Must be like syrup, thought Dolly, as she handed it over. Charmian, seated by the window, had retired to the sidelines. Dolly could see she was watching and wouldn't say much.

All three of them had been aware of noises from the next room, as of drawers being opened and shut. Soft noises of irritation from Kate, followed by one final loud bang of a drawer.

Kate came back into the room carrying a soft, brown leather sac with a zip top. It had a vaguely masculine air. The type of bag a man might carry his shaving gear in.

'Couldn't find it at first. I'd really forgotten where I'd put it.' She tossed it on the table. The bag was not new and had been well worn.

Sergeant Bister unzipped the bag. It fell into two separate halves, two little pouches lined with silk. On one side, nestling in newspaper, was a gun.

The gun. Kate's gun.

'Haven't touched it since India,' she said blithely. 'Didn't touch it then. You'll find the gun has not been used.'

Bister was studying the bag, carefully touching nothing. 'I'll have to take it away.'

'Of course.'

'Is that how you brought it from India?'

Kate nodded.

'Surprised it got through the checks.'

'It did. In my hand luggage. I think there was some sort of

crisis on that day, they were processing us through like sausages, or perhaps it's always like that at Delhi airport, but I'd sort of forgotten I had it. Otherwise I expect I would have dumped it somewhere.'

'And this side?' queried Bister, pointing to the leather bag. 'What was kept on this side?'

There was a crumpled nest of paper on the other side, a hollow shape that had once held something.

'So what was this side?' asked Bister smoothly. 'Did you have two guns, Miss Cooper?'

Kate, no longer, formality and distance restored. He didn't look such a jolly, easy young man any more, he looked quite stern.

'Of course not.'

'Are you sure?'

Kate said in a stiff voice, 'I am really quite sure I never did. I kept toilet bottles on that side.'

Sergeant Bister produced a large plastic bag into which he carefully inserted the leather sac, unzipped, almost untouched by him.

'What type is the gun, Sergeant?' asked Charmian.

'Looks like a neat blue Spanish pistol. Four-inch barrel,' he said, 'But I could be wrong. I'll know for sure when I've had a closer look.'

'And is that the type of gun that killed Nella Fisher?'

'Can't say at the moment, ma'am.' He turned to Kate. 'You won't be going away, will you, Miss Cooper?'

'No, certainly not,' she said, still stiff.

Charmian got up and stood by Kate in a protective way. It was Dolly who saw Bister and his accompanying and silent constable to the door. Then she came back, her face grim.

'Pretty lethal moment, wouldn't you say?' Dolly asked. 'I always knew he was a bastard.'

'I wouldn't say that,' said Kate. 'He was only doing his duty.' She dumped all the cups in the sink and ran water over them. 'Thanks for being here, both of you. But I'll be better on my own now. Thanks.'

Without waiting for an answer, she swung off to her bedroom and shut the door.

30

Thus dismissed, outside in the rain, Charmian and Dolly looked at each other without a word. No comments were necessary.

'How like Kate to forget where she'd put the gun.' Dolly started to climb to her own flat. 'You going to do anything about all this?' Her tone was doubtful, as if she was saying: But would it be wise?

'Damn it, I love the girl,' said Charmian. 'I don't know if I can.'

'I said he was a bastard,' said Dolly, as she stumped upstairs.

'I'd like to talk to you, Dolly,' Charmian called after her.

'Dinner here tomorrow, right?'

'Right.' And we'll get hold of Kate as well, was the promise behind the acceptance.

As Charmian got into her car, she realised she would have to take a hand, but it would need arranging. And probably scupper a career prospect of her own.

As she turned the car, she looked at the wide stretch of grass on which Nella Fisher had died. Now it looked peaceful, the turf very green and damp. She wondered what it had looked like on the day of the murder.

## CHAPTER THREE

# A look back at Monday September 18, then on to Friday October 6

Nella Fisher's body had been found on the scrubby piece of turf which stretched between the façade of the flats and the road. A small screen of evergreen bushes and newly planted trees curved in a semicircle in the middle of it, shielding the flats from the road.

It had also partly hidden the body of the dead girl.

She had rested among the laurel bushes, as if she had staggered there, mortally wounded, to die. Her body did not look arranged, but casual, as if she had dropped there, like a doll, without realising she was dead.

After the discovery, screens had been set around the area while photographs and measurements of an essential sort were taken and while the Scene of the Crime Officer settled the first moves in the investigation. At this stage the police did not anticipate any difficulty in finding the killer. They were sanguine of success. In this sort of killing, many people could usually name the likely murderer. They had only to locate those persons and they would be on their way.

They knew the girl. Her identity had soon been established by the library card in her pocket. It was a surprise to them that she could read and used a library, for they knew her as a troublesome character who used several aliases.

She drank, not a lot, but she seemed to have a weak head, and had been found drunk outside the museum and picture gallery in Nelson Street behind the railway station; she was suspected of using drugs, of passing them and possibly dealing in them.

But this was only police suspicion, nothing had been proved. She came from a family of criminous tendencies called, as it suited them, Fisher, Seaman, Waters or Rivers. They seemed to like an association with water of some kind, salt or fresh. This family, a widespread clan with many tentacles, came from the village of Cheasey in Buckinghamshire, now subsumed into the industrial complex of Slough, where it was widely known as the drug centre of the district. It also headed the lists for abortions, rapes, and muggings. You kept out of Cheasey if you could and avoided its denizens. Cheasey was reputed to have the highest percentage of criminals per hundred of population, outside some London boroughs. Some people blamed this on the nearness to Heathrow, others to inbreeding, pointing to the Cheasey dwarfs. These were an extended family of small, heavily bodied men (they ran to men) with short legs. But it had to be said that they were among the hardest working and most respectable inhabitants of Cheasey. They took jobs in the stables at Windsor and Ascot, worked in the circus at Slough, or ran errands as messengers almost like characters from *The Ring*. The neighbourhood of Cheasey accepted the Tiny Tippers – as they were called – without comment, as it accepted the Fisher-Rivers-Seaman clan. Dog did not eat dog in Cheasey. No one is perfect.

Nella's family had known the date of her funeral but had not wished to attend it. They didn't like funerals.

In spite of the police department's low opinion of Nella Fisher, who had certainly been a trouble to them, having bitten one police detective's nose (for sticking it where it wasn't wanted, to use her own phrase), the girl had made an attempt to get out of Cheasey ways. She had worked hard in her last year at the big school in Slough, and taken as many O-level exams as the teaching staff thought she might achieve. She passed English language and literature, but at a very low level, and failed history and social sciences. They were honourable failures, her teacher told her. Thus equipped with two low passes and two high failures, Nella attempted to get a place at the polytechnic in Windsor, but competition was high that year and she failed.

She was disappointed, and for some weeks she hung around

the buildings off Alma Road and near St Mary's Church, pretending she was a student. She had eaten in the student canteen and slipped into lectures as if she belonged there. She called herself Elly Seaman at the Poly and said her father was in the navy. She had a way of insinuating herself into other people's lives. At school she had hung about one of the teacher's house, not saying much, but sitting in his garden and playing with his dog. He had found it an oddly unnerving experience and on the advice of the Principal of the school had told her to keep away. The same thing had happened in the end at the polytechnic. She had been spotted as a cuckoo in the nest and warned off.

It was interesting that the educators felt a certain sympathy for Nella yet the police did not. They did, after all, get the rough side of Nella's character, because at the same time as she was seeking education she was also indulging in all those antisocial practices that brought her into contact with the police. The two activities seemed to go in tandem with her. In fact, the very day she attended her first lecture at the Poly – on 'The Origins of the Legal System, Anglo-Saxon England to Henry I' – and took notes with the best of them, was also the day she bit her first policeman.

By one of those coincidences which happen more often than they should, as if life believed in a theory of clusters, both Dolly Barstow and Kate Cooper had been in the polytechnic building at about the same time. Dolly was there on police business, investigating a string of petty thefts, and Kate, who was by training an architect and by nature a wandering scholar, was in the library reading books explaining Assyrian building styles.

They had never noticed Nella, but it was possible that she had observed them, since all three had eaten in the canteen.

On that misty autumn morning the girl's body was seen by a respected local inhabitant, Edward Dick, owner of the employment agency with all its allied activities, who was out walking his dog. She had already been found by the milkman on his round who had rung the police and was now waiting by his van for them to arrive. He was glad to see Mr Dick because the sight of so much blood had sickened him.

'Poor kid,' he said, 'poor kid.'

'Yes,' agreed Edward Dick, taking a look. He restrained

his dog who was at once pulling on the leash and beginning to whine.

He knew Nella Fisher. She had tried to get on the agency's books but because she seemed to have no skills which he could market he had turned her away.

But he knew her face.

Should he walk on, or stay here and support the milkman? Milk deliveries were going to be late today.

He decided to hurry on, ignoring the pleas of the milkman, and as he turned the corner of the road where he lived, he heard the arrival of the police car. There'd be an ambulance next, but they wouldn't move the body until the police surgeon had had a look. He knew a bit about police procedure, having served as an auxiliary police constable.

And goodness knows when the milkman would be released to deliver the milk.

This reminded Edward Dick that he would be short of milk himself, in that case, since he was one of the roundsman's customers, so he turned his feet towards a machine outside the grocer's that sold milk and took a carton home.

He lived above his own premises, Keyright Employment, which was two doors down from the grocer's, so he had not far to go.

As he let himself in, he reflected that he must have the girl's address on his files and that this might be information the police would want, but no doubt they had their own means of finding out where she had lived. She had told him her name was Ella Waters, although he later discovered that this was false.

He poured a bowl of milk for the dog and started to boil an egg for his own breakfast. Coffee came out of a jar and was easy. He had looked after himself since his mother died, finding a simple pleasure in the task. She had been a good cook, he was a poor one, but he liked his own food. He liked burned toast (which he got regularly every morning), hard-boiled eggs and lukewarm coffee.

Later that day, having put in a routine appearance in his office, he invented an excuse and drove to Nella Fisher's address, a backstreet in that undiscovered country between Windsor and Slough. It had once been a swamp, avoided by Anglo-Saxons, Vikings and Normans alike, only to be pioneered by the Victorians. There he stared, in what, he shamefacedly admitted, was idle curiosity, at the outside of the house.

All seemed quiet, although there must be some police activity going on inside. It was a nice little house, even if somewhat neglected and in need of paint. He had no idea in what conditions Nella had lived there or how many rooms she had had the use of. A bedsit, probably, Nella – or Ella – was a natural inhabitant of bedsit land, and might even have graduated to being completely homeless altogether or the inhabitant of a cardboard box.

Probably just as well she died, he thought. Nothing to look forward to but down.

Nearly three weeks after this, when the inquest was over and Nella's body released to be buried, the door of her room was still locked and the key in the police's possession.

But Charmian had got the use of it. She had been in the room once before, the day following the funeral, but she had not lingered. To get a key had required several telephone calls and some careful negotiation.

Now she wanted another look round.

She had permission to take an interest in the case. The phrase 'active interest' was not used, but the powers-that-be had no illusion that Charmian's interest would be anything less, but there was a tacit warning to her to be tactful.

She owed this permission to her friendship with Chief Inspector Father, who trusted her, and to the further fact that she had been offered the position of head of a special unit, newly created within the Force, and that it was desirable she accepted. A certain pressure had been put on Father from above.

Permission to stand in on the investigation into the death of Nella Fisher was a sweetener to Charmian to accept the new post. Of course, she wasn't allowed to prowl around on her own, she had a kind of watcher with her. But she had pulled more strings to get George Rewley.

Only afterwards did it strike her that maybe he too had been pulling strings to get that position for himself. He liked Kate Cooper, he liked her a lot.

Sergeant George Rewley, a colleague of Dolly Barstow's, had met Kate in Charmian's house over a year ago, and for some months their friendship had rolled along merrily, but then he had been called away to work with a drug control unit in the North of England, handing on advice and techniques, and when he came back somehow he had found it hard to get on terms with Kate again. She seemed to have drawn away. Not a man to stay around where he was not welcomed, he had thrown himself into his work and tried to forget her. Since they were a small CID force and he was in close contact with Dolly Barstow this was not easy, as he was obliged to hear talk of Kate, especially after their move to adjoining flats. He knew Dolly was curious about the split between them but she never asked questions.

Just as well, he told himself, because I wouldn't know the answer. He was usually good at reading between the lines, the unspoken conversations, the words that didn't get uttered. He had lost the knack with Kate Cooper. Perhaps he had liked her too much.

Now he stood with Charmian in Nella Fisher's room in the little sidestreet between Cheasey and Slough, geographically close to Eton and Windsor but socially a world apart.

They had met as if they had been working together for days, just a casual nod and 'Shall we get on with it?' from Rewley and a nod in response from Charmian.

She looked particularly unsmiling.

'How's Kate?' he asked as they plodded up the stairs. The house, a rented one, was currently unoccupied. The young married couple who had illegally sublet a room to Nella had moved out in a hurry when she was killed. No rent had been paid on either side for some time. The landlord was looking for them.

'All right. Back home.'

'Bearing up?' He felt he had to ask.

'Being Kate. Things seem to wash over her sometimes.'

'I know.'

'Bister kept her a long while for questioning, but the gun she handed over was not the gun that killed Nella so there wasn't much they could do but let her home.' Charmian added, 'Also her mother had laid on a team of very expensive lawyers.'

'I know that too.'

'And Jack, you know Jack?' Jack was Kate's father. 'He went down and threatened to beat up Bister if they didn't let his daughter alone. He was drunk, of course. I don't know why they didn't arrest him.'

'CI Father wanted to but Bister said it was beneath his dignity.' Charmian added, 'The leather bag with the gun seemed to have held a second object which looked alarmingly gun-shaped. Kate says it was some toilet article. But I know Father has having the whole object gone over for forensic traces.'

Rewley looked amused. 'All he's found so far is talcum powder. And tobacco.'

'Just tobacco?' asked Charmian, meaning no drug traces of any sort.

'Just tobacco. That's why he let her go.'

He opened the door of Nella Fisher's room. 'Here we are.'

'What a fug, still smells, doesn't it?' Charmian wrinkled her nose.

'Yes, she smoked a lot. Pot as well as virginia.' Rewley went over and opened a window. 'Not a girl who took a lot of care of her things,' he said as he looked about him.

They both stood silent for a moment, absorbing what they saw. Experienced police officers, both of them knew how important those first impressions of a room, a murder scene, or a person were. Sometimes you got a flash of insight.

'I'd like to get some sort of idea of Nella Fisher,' murmured Charmian.

The room had been untidy before the police team moved in to search and they had not improved things, emptying drawers and leaving the cupboard door swinging. The wall beside the bed was stuck with posters, pictures cut from magazines and scribbles of dates, addresses and telephone numbers. Nella had used it as a kind of jotting pad.

'They didn't find anything, though,' said Rewley. 'Nothing to help, that is. The late young lady kept no written records. No diary, no notes of whom she'd met and no letters.'

Charmian stooped to pick up a sweatshirt – it was torn but clean. 'You wouldn't expect it, would you?' she asked, moving round the room. She stepped over a pile of jeans and skirts, clean again even if creased.

'I'd expect a few letters,' said Rewley.

'Listen, I've had countless girls like Nella through my hands in my working life and they are not girls who write letters or get them.'

'I'd have expected her to have a bit of paper around – remember, she was a girl who tried to get herself educated – but there's nothing.'

Charmian stared at him. She went to a table by the bed.

'She's got pencils, though,' said Rewley, following her gaze. 'And a biro.'

'Are you telling me this room was searched before the police got here?'

Rewley shrugged. 'Could be.'

'What do Bister and Father think?'

'They haven't told me. But I wouldn't be surprised if they think what we do: that someone's had a look-see all on their own.'

'Mm.' Charmian sat down on the bed to consider. 'And do they think Kate was the searcher?'

'They will do if they can match a few prints.'

'I hope Kate hasn't been here,' said her godmother thoughtfully. She looked round the room, which was small and narrow. It contained nothing but a bed, a table and several chairs, with a cupboard against the wall for clothes. There were no facilities for washing or cooking, except a sink into which no water ran, so Nella must have shared the kitchen and the bathroom with her landlady. A mug with a sediment of what had once been coffee suggested that she did. Oddly, the sense of Nella was strong in the room and Charmian found herself thinking, Poor girl, poor girl.

Rewley went over to the window through which a fresh breeze was blowing together with a burst of rain. 'We are both fond of Kate, but do we both get the impression that Kate is not telling us all she knows?' He drew down the window with a bang.

'Yes,' said Charmian.

'Any idea what she's keeping to herself?'

'None. And I didn't know you'd spoken to her.'

'On the telephone,' he said. 'And she was not forthcoming. What about Dolly, she have any ideas? She's as close to Kate as anyone at the moment.'

'Dolly is on her knees thanking Providence she was away that night when Nella was killed and so keeping her clean.'

Charmian went over to the table where Nella's few household chattels were laid out: a knife and fork, two spoons, both plastic, the sort that come with bottles of medicine, and a small coloured tin that had been used as an ashtray by the look of it.

'And do you get the impression,' said Rewley, 'that our Dolly has something on her mind that she isn't talking about?'

It was a shrewd comment, and Charmian, who knew something, if not everything, of what was worrying Dolly, said nothing.

'So she is,' said Rewley.

He was skilled at reading faces and body movements. The only hearing member of his family, he had learned to lipread as they did, and to respond to almost imperceptible body movements. He had developed this skill at first as a kind of game, and now, as an aid to his profession. He kept quiet about his ability but word got around. He caused some alarm and even awe among his fellows, who seemed to attribute extrasensory powers to him, none of which he would have claimed for himself.

'She's talked to you,' he said.

'Not said a lot.'

Rewley laughed. 'If it's what I think it is that's worrying her, she wouldn't. Caution is our Dolly's second name.'

Charmian was surprised. 'I don't know if I want to go over this.'

'I doubt if Dolly suspects me of being on the take.'

'So you do know what it's about.'

'Just guessing.'

But with Rewley, guessing was brought to a fine art. It was more than just guessing, he had a way or arriving at a conclusion having noticed the markers on the path before anyone else.

Charmian wondered what signs he had detected. Probably the same as Dolly. And if Dolly Barstow and Rewley, then who else? Dolly was no doubt wise to be both nervous and on guard.

'Does Dolly think this murder has something to do with that business?'

'The idea has occurred to her,' admitted Charmian, picking up one of the spoons. 'And she doesn't like it.'

'She thinks that the man whom Nella claimed was threatening her and Kate, and whose identity she was prepared to divulge on payment, was a bent copper who killed Nella because she was a threat?'

'That's it. And she isn't too keen to talk about this theory.'

'Don't blame her.'

Charmian got up and moved closer to three photographs stuck on the wall where Nella could have seen them as she lay in bed.

One was of Kate with her mother which had appeared in a local newspaper. They were standing together at an exhibition of Annie Cooper's painting and pottery. It was a good photograph of them both, and Kate was easily recognisable.

The second was of Dolly Barstow. This too had been cut from a local newspaper, Charmian judged. From the look of it, and the woman on the platform with her, Dolly had been photographed giving a talk to a local women's group.

Next to these pictures was one of Chief Superintendent Charmian Daniels, leaving court after having given evidence. She had appeared particularly well groomed that day, and looked a forceful, elegant figure.

'If someone searched this room, they didn't touch the picture gallery,' said George Rewley. 'Want them taken down?'

'No, but I'd just like to know why I am there.'

'Because you knew the other two?'

'Perhaps.' Charmian turned away. 'That picture was taken after I'd given evidence in a porn case.' A big case, she had got a lot of publicity, because she had caught a really nasty ring of pederasts and child abusers. She had started getting obscene letters and porn in the post herself after that.

'It's a good photograph. Want to look around any more?'

'No, I think I've seen all I want to.'

Rewley shut the window, locking it into position. 'I don't

believe anyone has been into this room taking things out. Doesn't feel like it somehow. Maybe she kept any letters somewhere else.'

'Where, for instance?'

He shook his head. 'I don't know. I'll enquire around. But she might have been the sort that throws all letters away.'

'Not the impression you get from this room, is it? Oh well, let's go. Come round to Dolly's tonight. I'll see Kate is there as well. We can talk.'

On the way out, she trod on something that was sticking out from under the bed. She picked it up. It was a blood donor's card. Nella's name and the date of her last attendance at the hospital were inscribed. She had given blood on an afternoon not long before she had died.

It told her more about Nella Fisher than anything else she had seen. An empty room, but not an empty girl.

A girl with some heart. An eye to the main chance, not very clever, but she was struggling, and trying to offer what she had.

# CHAPTER FOUR

## *Earlier on Friday, October 6*

Dolly Barstow had seen, and got her hands on, a copy of
the outline of Nella Fisher's last two days which had been put
together by Sergeant Bister's team. He had thought this survey
important as establishing where she was and what she was doing.
In his method of work he liked to know the victim's movements.
Ten to one, he used to say, the victim and the murderer will have
met in that period. It gives you a start.

You needed a start with Nella, Dolly thought. The girl
had had a restless few days.

She ran her eye down the page. Just a catalogue, really.
Not much flesh on the bones.

The day before she died, Nella had taken a bus ride to
Windsor. It was not known what she had done there, but the driver of the small local bus, which ran in a shuttle around the town,
remembered that she had got on the bus at the Merrywick-Slough
roundabout, just before the motorway junction, and had ridden
in with him as far as Peascod Street where she had alighted.
She had waved to him and said 'See you on the way back,'
but he didn't remember seeing her again; still, he had gone off
duty at midday in any case. The relief driver did not remember
seeing Nella who could have walked back to Cheasey, or hitched
a ride. Her lodging was midway between the edge of Slough and
Windsor, on the bus route to Merrywick and just in the postal
district of Cheasey. She had never moved far from home.

There were a couple of sightings of someone who might be
Nella Fisher later that day. A family taking their children for
an outing reported seeing a girl who answered to her description

in the tea-room of the Windsor Safari Park. She was weeping but refused any offer of help. Didn't need any, she had said. Rebuffed, the Sadler family, mother, father and two children, had gone away. Strangely enough, weeping girls are not uncommon so it may not have been Nella.

On that same day, she had also popped into the polytechnic in Windsor for some food (she still ate in the canteen there in spite of having been turned out twice), then used her library ticket, taking out two books. They were found in her room after her death. Poetry and a novel by Thomas Hardy: *Tess of the d'Urbervilles*, a tragic story of the death of a young girl.

In the evening of that day, she had, if the observers were correct, drunk in several local pubs. How drink and drugs and a feeling for Thomas Hardy went together in the same girl was something that puzzled Sergeant Bister. Not Dolly Barstow, however. Poor kid, she thought. On the next day, which was September 17, the day of her death, she had taken the shuttle bus into Windsor once again.

She had been observed walking over Eton Bridge.

She had gone into an antique shop in the High Street.

She had been seen looking in the window of a bookshop.

She had walked to Merrywick and visited the Keyright Employment Agency where once again she was turned away. No job for such as she. But did she really want one? The owner, who was getting seriously fed up with Nella, doubted it.

Then she had walked back to Windsor and taken a train to Staines and then come back again. Since there seemed no reason for this journey there probably was not one, just filling in time. She had managed not to buy a ticket so no money had been spent. She had so very little of that and precious little time either . . .

She must have walked back to Merrywick because, of course, on this day she called on Kate Cooper once again.

And in the evening of this day, or possibly in the early morning of the next, she had been shot.

The post-mortem examination, when carried out, had revealed that she had died from just one shot which had penetrated the brain. Most of the bleeding had been internal. She had been a healthy young woman of some sexual experience, but she had never had a child.

There had been some difficulty in getting a post-mortem examination done, but after a short delay this had been effected. The reason for the delay was that Nella Fisher was HIV positive.

When Dolly read this she realised that Nella had known how little time was left to her.

Chief Inspector Father had also read the report on its completion and discussed it with Inspector Elman, now returned from his study course.

'Anything that comes out of Cheasey irks me,' admitted Father. 'Always trouble, that place. Still, poor kid, she didn't deserve what she got. We must clear this up soon, Fred.'

Cheasey rankled with him because earlier in his career he and Elman had had a failure. A lad called Gerry Henley, brother to the more infamous Jake Henley who ruled a small crime empire in Cheasey, had disappeared. Father would like to have got Jake Henley for it, but he had never succeeded. Never even found the body. It rankled.

He had initialled Bister's report and passed it on to those needing to see it.

Dolly Barstow photocopied the sheets and prepared to hand them over to Charmian Daniels, first clearing this with Chief Inspector Father.

# CHAPTER FIVE

## *The evening of Friday, October 6*

Maid of Honour Row, to which Charmian drove after leaving
Rewley outside Nella's lodgings on the edge of Slough, did not
look its best when the rain was pouring on it. Its neat little
Victorian face needed sunlight to light up the shining brass on
the doorknockers and reflect the colour of the flowers in the
windowboxes. Charmian had planted her boxes with bulbs for
the spring: daffodils, tulips and tiny iris. She cheated for the
winter by putting in a few artificial geraniums, red and white.
Her neighbour next door, an elderly widower, suspected they
were artificial but had never been able to prove it.

Charmian knew of these suspicions and took a delight in
deceiving Mr Elcho by pretending to water them occasionally.

'Always in bloom those geraniums,' he had said, eyeing
them with doubt.

'A very good sort. Everlasting Red,' she had answered.
'I recommend them.'

She rated it a weakness on her part but she enjoyed the
game. She thought he did, too, and that he would catch her
out in the end. It was a prospect he looked forward to no doubt,
because he did not like her cat Muff, nor the dog Benjy who
also belonged to her, but who lived round the corner with her
friends Winifred Eagle and Birdie Peacock, making occasional
home visits. A woman who worked in London every day could
not really look after a loving young dog, but liked to see him
when she could. Say the odd weekend.

It would be one of Benjy's home weekends this coming one,
she reflected, as she returned to the house after seeing Nella's

46

room. She must warn Muff. The cat was no dog-lover but was good at training dogs and Benjy was learning the rules: keep quiet, keep out of my way and remember this is cat territory.

Charmian sat in the car for a moment before she got out. She had that strange feeling that someone was watching her. She looked in the driving mirror, studying the road behind her.

No one there, the little street was empty. No one in the gardens of the terrace of Victorian red-brick houses that lined one side. On the other side a belt of trees could have hidden anyone.

She got out and walked across. The rain was steady now, dripping on the trees, making them droop and move sadly. The raindrops slithered to the ground with soft plashes. She could smell the rain on the leaves.

Nothing to be seen, but a faint movement at the back of the belt of trees. It might be the wind, which was mounting with every passing minute.

Well, it was my imagination, she thought.

But she did not blame herself for her super-caution. There had been times lately when the price of safety had been extreme vigilance.

She had been engaged, with several other officers from different Forces, in an investigation covering two continents. Their cover had been a conference on inner-city crime, a conference of which this group had seen little, being otherwise engaged. Of this investigation Charmian had been the co-ordinator and keeper of the records. A dangerous job, and if Kate and Dolly thought her visit to New York had been holiday, then they were wrong. Dolly probably guessed better.

But that task was successfully behind her now, and she ought to be able to relax. Relax and consider the new position that had been offered to her. It was a job she ought to want, but she wasn't sure if she did; it would anchor her in Windsor and she did enjoy London. She liked the excitement of a big city. But it was a good job.

Her mind went back to a scene which had taken place a few weeks ago.

A lunch party in a white-panelled room overlooking a green quadrangle in one of Oxford's brighter colleges: St Jude's.

Known locally as Judas College, having been one of the first to admit women to a former male cloister.

There had been four people present at the lunch, a small party, she was surprised to see. The host, Dr David Lemmer, had casually introduced the other two men as Dick Helling and Marcus Frost.

Charmian had been pleased to be asked to the luncheon by David, a friend and contemporary at Eton of Humphrey whom she might, just, marry. Flattered even, you could say, but when she got there, puzzled.

'Thank you.' She accepted the very dry sherry which was famous at Judas as an aperitif. (Anything else would be vulgar, although undergraduates had been known to drink gin, and a famous politician had once asked for gin in his sherry.) A quick flick through her memory produced the card which said that Marcus Frost was a baronet, third generation, and in the Home Office. She considered this fact while refusing a second glass of wine.

Dick Helling, she recognised as someone she had seen before. She ate her lobster thermidor while maintaining a brisk conversation on the subject of horse racing, about which she knew very little but which, she had observed, dons found a fashionable and pleasing subject, and trying to remember where she had seen him before.

Over the *crème brûlée*, a difficult dish to negotiate if you are the chief guest and must dig into the skating rink of sugar first, she remembered who he was.

Over the coffee, she realised she was being vetted for a job. Over the brandy, she knew what it was: head of a new unit which was to control all documentation of crime.

She knew enough of the world to realise that such a department would be exceedingly powerful. The initials SCRADIC were being dropped into the conversation.

So it already had a name?

She had left that luncheon party in a thoughtful mood. Why did they want her? Did they think she would be easy to control? Or was it some devious trick to sidetrack her? It behoved a woman to be cautious, even suspicious in a male world. Watch your step, girl, was written on every careerwoman's heart, and covered everything from the loss of virginity and childbirth to learning how to type. No, it was a good position of real power. So it must be a genuine compliment.

The weeks had passed but no definite offer had come. Other people were obviously being considered. But recently, she had begun to get definite hints that she was the chosen candidate.

All this was in her mind as she stood in Maid of Honour Row, listening and watching for one more moment. Nothing to see. If anything it was quieter, except for the rain which was heavier than ever.

But as she was turning away, she noticed something else. A faint, a very faint smell of cigarette smoke.

No, not cigarette, cigar. Or, at any rate, something heavy, scented and rich.

She pushed her way through the trees and shrubs until she came to the road on the other side. But there was nothing and nobody.

That was probably a silly thing to do, Charmian, she told herself, as she walked back round by the road. If you'd met someone there, then you might have been in trouble.

As it was, all she had done was to get thoroughly wet.

The house seemed warm and welcoming, smelling faintly of lavender polish. While she was away, a house-cleaning team had come in and refurbished the house from top to bottom. Kate had given her this as a homecoming present. Kate could be so generous. Also difficult, elusive and tricky.

Charmian hung up her raincoat; she was careful with her clothes, as only someone who had been hard-up in youth was likely to be. Then she went into the kitchen to make some tea.

This time last year Kate had been living with her here, now the house felt empty without her. But it had never been an arrangement that was meant to last, they had both known that.

As the kettle boiled, the cat Muff strolled into the kitchen, mouthing a silent greeting. She drank a saucer of milk on the table while Charmian sipped her tea, putting a hand out occasionally to stroke the cat's head. Muff arched her neck in reply.

Charmian poured some more tea. It was a bad business, the way Nella Fisher had been shot.

No one had heard the shot, no one had seen the murderer come or go. Even the motive for the killing was unknown, unless you connected it with the girl's mixture of warning and threat to Dolly and Kate.

Nella's behaviour itself was a puzzle. People don't behave like that, do they?

Ibsen, you should be living at this hour, thought Charmian. People do anything and everything and their motives are not always clear-cut, even to themselves. Sometimes, perhaps, least of all to themselves.

What seemed to be established was that Nella had got hold of some sort of a story, that this story involved a threat to either Kate or Dolly. Possibly Dolly was the victim. And Nella had wanted money for the story.

But Nella herself had turned into a victim.

She was a victim and she needed money.

These seemed to be the only two hard facts you could know about Nella at this moment.

Muff yawned delicately and leapt from the table. Charmian rose also to telephone Dolly who must be told about another guest for dinner.

'Dolly? I've asked George Rewley to look in tonight. That's all right, I hope? I think we all ought to talk.'

'Oh sure.' But there was restraint in Dolly's voice. 'He's welcome.'

'That's not how you sound.'

'Oh well, you might as well know. Before he met Kate last year, there were passages between us. Nothing much, but there you are. It just makes for little difficulties occasionally. On the whole, I've been avoiding him. Except for work. Can't avoid him there.' But as it happened their paths had not crossed in cases lately. Luck? Or the careful management of his life which she knew George Rewley was capable of? I'm not a lucky lady, she said to herself. Not lucky at all. Then she laughed.

'What are you laughing at?' asked Charmian.

'Myself. Forget it. I'm always glad to see George. He's a decent bloke. And he sees further into the wood than most people. Kate is coming, I managed to persuade her. She's inclined to hide at the moment, which isn't like her.'

Not quite true, thought Charmian. Kate could not only hide, she could run away, and had done that more than once in the past. She could disappear, leaving a hole in your life, only to come back, taking things up as if she had never been away. It was either endearing or maddening according to your mood of the moment.

'She's got something on her mind,' she said to Dolly.

'So come early, before the others, so we can talk.'

Always my intention, thought Charmian, as she went to change her clothes.

Learning about what to wear had been a late development in her life, and had come when she began to have enough money to spend on good clothes. As a hard-up student, clothes had been bought in an Oxfam shop or had been a present from her mother at Christmas, then later, as a young career police officer, there had never seemed time, not to mention money, to think about what she wore. She had tried, of course, to look well dressed, especially during her brief and troubled marriage to a man much older than herself, but it was not until her career flowered that she had allowed herself to buy expensive clothes. Now she knew her style, and chose well-cut, simple clothes in warm colours. The girl from Glasgow, who still lurked inside her, had been surprised and even shocked at what those simple clothes cost. But she enjoyed wearing them.

Now she reached inside her wardrobe for a trouser suit designed by Jean Muir. Names came and went in fashion, this year an Italian was the one to buy, last year it had been a Japanese, next year, who knew? But some names were classic and went on.

The dark blue trousers went with a soft tomato-coloured silk shirt which ought to have clashed with her reddish hair but, marvellously, did not.

The old Charmian would have worn plain shoes, the new Charmian knew to wear a decorative pair from Maud Frizon. Humphrey had taught her about shoes. He had an instinctive feeling for the good and the expensive. An education, she told herself, but wondered if she wanted to marry an educationalist.

At present he was working in Geneva, from which city he telephoned frequently, on one of those nameless quiet security missions that took up his life, so the relationship was on hold.

And she herself had had this offer of a top position in the new regional unit to be formed around Windsor, so she might be leaving London. Not that the move would necessarily cut her off from Humphrey who had a small country house across the county boundary in Oxfordshire.

She had promised to go to Geneva for Christmas. Might or might not, she told herself. If she said it often enough, she might come to know what she really wanted to do.

Freedom, and she believed she had freedom, could be illusory if you did not know where you wanted to go.

The telephone rang on the table by her bed. She finished putting on her lipstick before answering it.

'Hello?'

'Miss Daniels? Charmian Daniels? Is that you?'

A deep voice, but with odd higher notes. Unnatural, somehow, as if control was being exercised over it, a made-up voice. Not a voice she knew, she answered cautiously.

'Speaking. Who is it?'

'Sorry. I'll call later.'

'Who are you?'

No answer, the line went dead.

Charmian put the receiver down, and went back to her dressing table. Like many people in the public eye she knew what it was to get odd, cranky calls, and for this reason she had an unlisted number.

But there were ways of getting her number. People, friends, passed it on. You couldn't hide. Life did not offer dugouts.

If, as seemed likely, this was one of those crank calls, she knew better than to take it personally. Just a floating patch of general malevolence settling on her.

But not agreeable, not to be encouraged. Well, she could always get her number changed. Again.

She was buttoning on her Burberry when the telephone rang once more. She debated ignoring it, then went back to answer it. She lowered her voice and spoke quietly.

'George Rewley here,' said a cheerful voice. 'Is that you, Charmian? Doesn't sound like you.'

'It's my telephone voice.'

'I like the other one better. I know we're going to meet in a few minutes, but I've picked up a bit of information. A witness has come forward who claims to have seen someone walking down the road in Merrywick with Nella just about the time she was shot.'

'That could be crucial.'

'I didn't want to talk about it in front of Kate.'

'No, I see that.'

'I don't know any more. Who the witness was and what was seen.'

'How did you find out?'

'I heard Bister talking about it to Fred Elman. He shut up when he saw me.'

'Thanks for telling me. See you soon. I'm just off to Dolly's now.'

As she got to the door the girl from Glasgow stirred inside her again, and she stopped to take off the pretty shoes and tuck them under her arm while she put on a sturdier pair. The red-and-blue suede shoes were not made for walking in the rain or for driving. Put them on when you get to Dolly's, said her severe internal preceptor, whose voice, she had to admit it, sounded exactly like her mother's.

Such pretty shoes and so expensive, one couldn't spoil them. She put her foot down and drove swiftly to Merrywick.

There was a lot of traffic around tonight. There was a musical festival taking place in Windsor Castle and everyone was going. She could have been there herself. Humphrey had sent her tickets for several concerts, together with advice on which were likely to be the best performances. The educationalist again?

Someone had put a spray of flowers on the spot where Nella had fallen. One of her family? Why didn't they come to her funeral? thought Charmian. Someone ought to find out.

Dolly must have been waiting for her, since she opened the door at once.

'Not late, am I?' Charmian took off her raincoat. Wet again, this was the wettest autumn ever. 'Tell me, why didn't the girl's family come to her funeral? She did have one, I've read the notes on her.'

'I don't know why.'

'I think it would be worth finding out.'

'You think it's important?' Dolly was pouring some wine.

'Unexplained facts often are.'

'That's too sophisticated for me,' said Dolly in a good-humoured voice.

The two women, in spite of their age difference, were good friends. Dolly was very careful to address Charmian by her rank in the world outside, but within her own home, she relaxed.

Not that she was notably relaxed at the moment, as Charmian saw. 'We've got about ten minutes, so shall we start?'

'Kate's always late,' said Dolly.

'And Rewley's not.'

'Right, well, I'll just plunge in. I happened to be eating a quick meal in a wine bar, well a pub, in fact, in Cheasey. I'd had a witness to see in Slough and stopped at this place on the way home. I won't even say which one. I saw a police officer, uniformed branch, not CID, not one of my lot, but I knew the face. This officer was in company I should not care to keep myself.'

'That's part of the job,' suggested Charmian.

'I know. And one of the dangers. Things brush off.' She thought for a moment. 'I'll use the name Roger.'

'Not Roger's real name, I take it?'

'Nothing like.'

'I knew the man Roger was with. He's well-known for being behind a porn video ring. We've never been able to get him, although he has been in court once or twice. I also knew that there had been a raid on one of his warehouses the week before, from which he had walked away clean. The place was empty. Even being repainted. Couldn't have been cleaner.'

'And Roger would have known this raid was to take place?'

Dolly nodded. 'I can't say I saw any money pass between them. I think they would have been cleverer than that. Or Roger would. But I believe it did.'

Charmian drank some wine. 'Were you seen?'

'I thought not. But from something that happened afterwards I think I could have been.' Dolly ceased in her walking up and down the room. 'It was while you were away. Someone broke all the windows in my car.'

'A vandal?'

Dolly shrugged. 'So I thought at first. Then I came back here and some of the glass had been shoved through my letterbox. I can't prove the connection but . . . ' she paused.

'But you're nervous.' Charmian drank her wine. 'Do you think Roger did it?'

'Oh no, far too canny. Nor Mr Magister, that's not his name either, the porn king. He just hired someone. And would do so again.'

'How does Nella Fisher come into this?'

'I wasn't sure if she did at first. But I found out that Nella worked for a few weeks in that pub. I think that's where she heard the threats she claimed she listened to.'

'And was killed by a hired gun?'

Dolly said: 'No. I think Roger did that.'

'Have you got a reason for thinking so?'

'Not exactly a reason, just a feeling. I believe there might be something personal as well,' said Dolly slowly. 'Just something Nella said. As if the person she was telling tales about knew her. They had a past together.'

She hesitated. 'And there is something else. Something I just learned today. We have a witness who saw Nella that night with another person. I think they came here together. I think that other person was Roger.'

'Would Nella go for a walk with Roger?'

'Yes, because I think Roger is someone she might, in a funny way, trust.'

'Nella did not sound the sort to trust a policeman, especially one she knew to be corrupt.'

'But I think she might trust this one,' said Dolly slowly. 'Or just so far to be off her guard for long enough.' If Roger had killed her.

'Who told you about this witness?' asked Charmian, not letting on that she had already heard.

'Tom Bister. He sort of let it out.'

'Can this witness describe the person with Nella?'

'Not really,' said Dolly. 'Light wasn't good. Or that's the story. Not sure if I believe it.'

'But he or she knows it was Nella, and could see her well enough?'

'That's about it. The pair moved into the shadows.'

'Did this witness know Nella?'

'Certainly seen her before,' said Dolly carefully.

Why did Charmian get the impression that Dolly was keeping something back?

Because she is, said the voice of reason inside her, Dolly is not telling everything. Nor is Kate. Probably not George Rewley and certainly not Sergeant Bister, who had 'let it' out to Dolly and who may even have meant Rewley to hear what he said about the new witness. And for that matter, she herself was not being totally open.

'Who is this witness?' she demanded.

'A police officer,' said Dolly reluctantly. 'Off duty.'

The same story that George Rewley had just passed on, but Dolly had added another detail: she knew the witness.

'This witness has been a bit slow in coming forward.'

'Been on a package holiday and out of touch,' said Dolly.

'And might have the same reason that you have for keeping quiet?'

'I don't think so,' said Dolly. She had a careful, blank look on her face.

Dolly had the report on Nella Fisher's last few days on her desk, but so far she had not given it to Charmian. She was just about to do so when the doorbell rang.

Kate and George Rewley arrived together, although quick to explain that it was coincidence.

'I just walked up the stairs and there was George,' said Kate.

'Nice place you've got here, Barstow.' George produced a bottle of wine from his raincoat pocket.

'Still raining, is it?' Dolly looked at the wine label. Sancerre. He knew what she liked. It would go with the meal too: sole in cream sauce with a spinach roulade. She hadn't cooked it, but she knew where to shop to find food like that.

'Will it ever stop?'

They gathered in the big living room where Dolly had lit the gas fire. Before they could get too cosy, and forget what they were there for, Charmian said, 'We're going to talk over all the events surrounding Nella Fisher's death as far as we know them.'

George Rewley sat in a corner of the room, quietly watchful, as was his way. He wouldn't talk unless asked a question, but he was observing their faces, their hands, and how they placed their feet. You could tell a lot that way. The only member of his family who could hear, he lipread and observed body signs as a way of life. He noticed and admired Charmian's shoes. Kate was wearing white trainers, a bad sign in her case, he thought, since they no longer represented the kind of high fashion Kate went for; it meant she wasn't trying.

Charmian started the proceedings.

'It's an odd tale. Dolly has told me what she thinks is behind Nella's visits to you. She has even told me why she thinks there might be some truth in the warnings that Nella gave her, that Dolly herself might be booked as a victim of violence.'

'Still might,' said Dolly.

'So what about you, Kate? What did you make of Nella's threat and tales? Did you believe them?'

'She struck me as being desperate. But I don't know why. She wanted money,' said Kate. 'I think she'd have threatened anything. Told any lies to get it.'

'But she thought she had something to sell. Some bit of information. Did she tell you more than she did Dolly?'

Kate shrugged. 'She didn't say much. She told me a policewoman might be under threat. She knew Dolly was my friend. I didn't really believe a lot of what she said.'

'Let's go over the evening of Nella Fisher's death again.' Charmian looked at Dolly and Kate. 'You two can talk and I will listen.'

George Rewley was watching as well as listening; she did not forget that.

'Can we talk over the soup?' asked Dolly. She was a good cook but a nervous one. 'Nothing will spoil the soup but the next course is tricky.' She had bought a prepared soufflé to go before the sole but it had to go in the oven and come out and be eaten according to a strict timetable.

Over the soup, which was thick and spicy and hot, they talked. Dolly first.

She had worked all day on a shoplifting case, nabbed the old queen who was responsible for a considerable loss from a furniture store ('You wouldn't think you could lift a sofa, two armchairs and a television set, would you?'), taken statements and got the prisoner his solicitor. Then she had come home to change for an evening out. The Stafford Hotel. Yes, she had witnesses. She had driven herself, and she thought Kate had seen her go off. Just from the window, they had not spoken that day. At the hotel, of course, there were many people who would remember her. The evening of September 17 had been a festive occasion for her until she heard afterwards what had happened.

Kate bore out what Dolly had said, Yes, she had seen her friend depart, but apart from that they had not met all day. Just a wave from the window. She herself had spent a quiet and solitary day. A fit of sneezing in the morning had made her suspect a cold coming on (Kate took her health seriously) so she had stayed home. The post had delivered a parcel of books she had ordered from the London Library to which she had devoted the day. The evening had been quiet and she had gone to bed early. No, she would not have heard the shot, since she slept at the back, well away from the grass where Nella had died.

The two stories dovetailed. The mood of the party was quiet as they ate Dolly's good food and drank the wine that Rewley had brought. Over the meal they carefully did not talk about the murder.

And as if to forestall any more talk, Kate soon rose and said she was tired and would be off. Dolly did not try to detain her or the others. Instead she stood up and went for their coats.

As they prepared to go, Charmian said in a low voice to Rewley, 'Well?'

'They are both lying.'

'Dolly too?'

'Certainly Dolly.'

58

'Damn.' Charmian took a deep breath. 'So what was the area of the lying? Can you pinpoint it?'

'For both girls, when they were talking about each other. I think they did meet that day. And in addition, for Kate, there is the evening. She was very tense about that.'

'Well, you can tackle Dolly. I will shake Kate and see what drops out.'

She cornered Kate on the stairs outside Dolly's flat. 'Before you go, there's some questions I want to put to you, Kate.'

'Ask away.'

'You're keeping something back.' It was a statement, not a question. 'Just say yes or no.'

Kate was silent.

'All right, I take that as yes. But I knew it, anyway. In some ways, you're a poor liar, Kate. I'll get there, Kate, I'll find out. But we'll leave that for the moment. The other question is this: Did you go out of your flat that night, and take a walk?'

This time Kate was quick to answer. 'No, I didn't set foot outside. Not once.'

'Can you prove that?'

Kate shook her head. 'No one was with me. But I have a sort of proof. I made a telephone call about eleven o'clock. Maybe a while before. I watched the television news and then rang.'

'Who did you telphone?'

'My father.'

Charmian believed her. In any case, it could be checked and she doubted if Kate would offer a lie which could easily be shown up. But to her mind, it was an interesting call.

'Well, let's get back to what you are hiding, Kate. I know you have a temper, I know you can blow up at people. But you aren't stupid, and you don't do it without a reason.'

Kate kept quiet.

'I'm waiting.'

'You're rotten sometimes, Charmian.'

'Trust me.'

The words started to come out, as if a bandage had been taken off a wound. 'Nella had this tale she wanted to tell me. Share with me, she said.' Kate gave a sad little laugh. 'About a

59

man obsessed with a policewoman. Not nicely obsessed. She'd insulted him. He wanted to get even.'

Charmian remembered Dolly's story. 'Jack?'

Kate put her head down. 'I thought Nella meant my father. I think she wanted me to believe it was my father. It was then I hit her.'

'Did you talk to Dolly about this, talk on that day?'

Was this the lie that Rewley had detected? If they had talked that evening, then it might provide the motive that Bister and Elman were probably looking for.

Kate stiffened. 'No. Certainly not.'

Another lie? I could do with a lie detector, Charmian thought, but Kate probably knows how to sidetrack one. Or would learn.

Two different versions, Dolly's and Kate's, two different attackers, a corrupt policeman and Jack Cooper. Only one victim envisaged: Dolly Barstow.

But not the one actually killed. The girl who died was Nella Fisher.

Not a bad girl, she gave her blood. Yet she was not mourned by her family.

As she drove home, Charmian continued this train of thought. Why had no one from Nella's family come to her funeral?

The little house was quiet and welcoming; in its hundred and fifty years of history it had known many comings and goings, births and deaths, tragedies and rejoicing, and its message was that you live through it.

Muff, the cat, pushed open the cat flap and welcomed Charmian. Then she ate a saucer of fish, preceded Charmian to the bedroom, where she sat purring. Outside, in the bushes across the road, someone had trodden on her tail, a painful and ruffling experience. There's a nasty foot out there, she could have said, but words were not her medium.

Charmian lay in bed and looked at the ceiling. She had never felt quite at ease with Jack Cooper. But he was Kate's father and Annie's husband. Annie was her best friend. She had been at their wedding.

The marriage had been turbulent and no one could call Jack easy. But a murderer?

Then the other story. Dolly's tale about the corrupt policeman. Roger, so-called. Roger might feel a strong desire to attack Dolly, if Dolly looked like being a threat, and had humiliated him. Nella had claimed he did. But why kill Nella?

Why should Roger, whoever Roger was, kill Nella?

There was one more puzzle: Dolly's story, as told by Dolly, did not include any incident in which she had insulted and belittled Roger.

The two stories seemed to merge in a puzzling way.

She wondered if George Rewley would telephone with news of a breakthrough with Dolly, but the telephone remained silent.

She considered telephoning Dolly herself . . . She reached out a hand . . . but Dolly had her answering machine on. Permanently on, probably.

In her own flat, Dolly Barstow turned off her tape recorder. 'That's it, then.'

She had taken the precaution of taping the whole evening's conversation. In her present mood, she trusted no one and nothing except her own quick senses. She wasn't going to unburden herself to George Rewley.

She went back to their dialogue just before he left. 'Come on, Dolly, what are you keeping back?'

'Your imagination is working overtime, George.'

What she was not telling was that she had seen Nella Fisher in the road outside the flats in Merrywick and she herself had seen the police officer she called Roger following her. That was something she was keeping quiet about.

There was guilt as well, she ought to have done something about it. That was something she was keeping to herself, too.

Dolly's telephone had rung three times after the party had left. Once it was Kate, once Charmian, but the third caller had left no message.

She put the chain on the front door and went to bed. Tomorrow she would let Charmian see the report on Nella Fisher's last days.

Kate was not asleep, and did not wish to sleep. She had tried to telephone Dolly but, like Charmian, got the answering machine.

The sleep of all three women was troubled, Charmian's most of all. She did not like the idea of an accidental or even a substitute victim. There had to be a reason why Nella Fisher was killed.

It all came back to the wild figure of Nella Fisher herself. Know the victim, Charmian told herself, and you might learn who was the killer.

Outside, the man in the bushes watched her bedroom window. His ankle stung a little where that damned cat had managed to get through trouser and sock. He was in a bad mood anyway.

Or was it a good mood? Hate could be a pleasure and mingle very strangely with love so that he sometimes hardly knew what he felt himself.

About the killing. That one first. This one next. But it ought to have been the other way round.

# CHAPTER SIX

## Friday, October 6, for another group of people

Woman Police Sergeant Margery Foggerty was a comfortably built woman whose uniform fitted her with some snugness. She was a motherly, kindly figure who was quite content to fill the policewoman's traditional role of looking after women and children in distress. She preferred it that way, and had no ambitions to enter the CID. Her reward had been a steady, gentle course of promotion. She had reached her peak, and she knew it; if she stayed on, then she would retire in ten years' time as a sergeant. But she enjoyed her work, knew she was suited to it, and was happy with her house and her own society. If she had a grumble it was that the financial rewards were not great. Still, you did what you could.

She had thought long and hard before coming forward with her story about seeing Nella walking with someone. Finally, she had decided that she really had better speak out. There could be other witnesses.

She might have been seen herself and been recognised. Her sister and brother-in-law had a house in Merrywick which she visited regularly, especially since their marriage was breaking up and divorce looked on the cards. Margery did not want Muriel to divorce, she was not the sort of woman to be thrown on the hard, cold world since there was no sign that she could support herself. Frank might not be an ideal husband, no one pretended he was, but he was Muriel's and she'd better keep him. She had known what he was like when she married him and he hadn't changed with the years. There were no ideal husbands anyway, and Muriel had not been an ideal wife.

Foggerty had been married herself, to another police officer, but police marriages are under constant strain and they had parted fairly amicably some five years ago. He was a Superintendent now in another force and had remarried. She was not jealous of his success, she had created her own life and enjoyed what she got from it. Holidays, a good car, a nice little house. At heart she knew she did not want to share.

Especially with Muriel, who had better stay where she was.

Margery had been on her way from telling her sister this blunt truth, and mopping her up after she heard it, when she had seen Nella Fisher. Nella was known to her and she was known to Nella and no love lost. It was a pity they had ever met.

Foggerty – she preferred to be called this at work – had served as WPC in Cheasey, Nella's home village, a sobering experience for a young woman from which she had learned a lot, not all of it good. For which she did not blame herself; life in Cheasey was a kind of disease and you were bound to pick up a scrap of infection.

As a result of this two years of service, she knew the Fisher clan, one of the principal pillars of the criminal community of Cheasey. She had been responsible for putting several of them inside. Cousins of Nella, as she remembered . . . or possibly even more closely linked. The relationships in that extended family did not bear thinking about. Incest was nothing out of the way.

By training and by natural aptitude, Margery Foggerty had a good memory for faces, so that she had recognised Nella easily when she had seen her about Windsor and Slough. Not to put a name on her perhaps, not to be able to say: That's Nella Fisher. But she knew that she came from Cheasey and that she was probably a Fisher girl. Names were always tricky in that outfit, kind of interchangeable. Positive identification came later, after a few questions asked around. And then later, Nella, who had recognised Foggerty too, had tried a little clumsy blackmail; she had underestimated Foggerty there and got nothing for her pains.

Nevertheless, the death by shooting of Nella Fisher had

been a tremendous shock. A real blow in the gut. Put her off her food, and that took some doing.

It was when sitting in the canteen and realising that bacon, egg and chips were not sliding down as happily as usual, that she made her decision.

She had just come back from a short period of leave during which she had flown out for a little holiday in sunny Spain (on her own, but she knew how to pick up the right company when she wanted it), during which time she had been able to push the problem of Nella to the back of her mind.

To the back, but not out of it. The trouble with being a woman, she decided, was that, do what you will, you had a feeling heart. More than a man ever had. Nella had been a nuisance while alive, and looked like being even more of a nuisance now she was dead. Margery Foggerty moved her bacon and eggs aside. They were cold as it happened, they had got cold while she thought things out. Her cup of tea was cooling also, and she detested lukewarm tea.

Bister was sitting at a table across the room. She got herself a mug of hot tea and walked over. Confession time.

She passed Dolly Barstow on her way across: they were not buddies.

Bister looked up at her as she sat down at his table. His eyes had their usual cold, clear light. Pale-blue eyes changing to grey in certain lights were never friendly eyes.

'It was nice in Spain,' said Foggerty settling herself into her seat. Her flesh overflowed a bit so it took some doing. 'I was sorry to get back.'

'Glad you enjoyed it.'

'Things seem to have been happening while I was away.'

'Such as?' asked Bister without interest.

'Murder on the patch. Nella Fisher.'

'You were around when she was killed.'

'I went off the next day.' Foggerty took a sip of her tea. This wasn't going well. As usual, Bister knew all the details you hoped he had forgotten. He had been a nuisance to her before.

'So what have you come to tell me?'

'What makes you think I'm telling?' said Margery over her mug.

65

'I've got nothing to tell you, so that if you haven't, there's no conversation.'

Such charm, thought Foggerty. Slays me.

Her eyes followed the figure of Dolly Barstow as she went through the swing doors and down the corridor. Barstow was a pal of that Charmian Daniels woman which always put her on the inside track. Daniels was about the same age as Foggerty but infinitely far above her in status. Life was very unfair.

There was another side, however, her thoughts rolled along comfortingly: she may have better pension rights, but I bet I've got more capital. Margery had been both careful and canny. Her stomach served her a rolling heave, to remind her that it too was here on business.

'I've come to tell you something,' she said, leaning forward.

Bister had finished his meal and was ready to go. 'I've got quite a dossier on Fisher. So if you've come to tell me anything about her home life, how she was in care at the age of eight, on probation at thirteen, and was missing for six months when she was fourteen, no one ever did discover where she was, don't bother, I've got all that and don't need more.' Unlike Charmian Daniels he did not believe that knowing more about the emotional or psychological life of a victim was a key to what had happened to them. Dates, motives and opportunity was what solved crimes, he thought, together with the forensics. Heaven forbid he should forget those. He and Inspector Fred Elman had set up their MIRIAM – major incident room – in a church hall in River Walk, Merrywick. He was on his way there now. 'And I don't want intuition, either.'

'As if I would.'

No, silly of him, Foggerty was not one for the sensitive approach to detection. Besides Sergeant Margery Foggerty he sometimes felt thin-skinned himself, while admitting that the tough and unsavoury work she had to do was well done by her. No obscene sexuality or act of bestiality did she flinch from, and she would rescue those she could. Not with any love, but efficiently.

All the same, he did not like her.

'No, I don't know why I didn't tell you this before I went away . . . ' She gave a shake of her head. 'But it sort of got pushed out of my thoughts by that kid that buried her twin brothers in a sandpit, little beast. Mind you, we got them out, but one of them might be brain damaged.'

Bister waited, more or less patiently.

Foggerty's stomach gave another sharp contraction, reminding her they were both here on business. Wonder if I've picked up some bug in sunny Costa Brava, she thought, knowing it was just nerves. Better get on with it instead of wittering on about the Brown twins who probably had deserved what they got. She was on the sister's side there. Girl children always got lumbered, and as the kid said, she was only putting them in a safe spot while she went away to play.

'I saw the girl in Merrywick that night, on that road and not far from where she was killed.'

'What was she doing?'

'Just walking.'

'What were you doing?'

'I was walking too. I was on my way back from my sister. She lives in a road near there. I saw Fisher in the distance.'

'But you recognised her?'

'Oh sure, she always wore the same sort of thing, a dark, black kind of sack over black jeans. I don't think she had anything else.' The clothes had suited her in her lost-girl way. Never pretty, Nella had an appeal like a rain-drenched kitten.

Bister did not want to reject the offering but he didn't see what it added. 'Was the light good?' he asked thoughtfully.

'No, not very, it was raining.'

Not much help really, he thought. 'Well, thanks for telling me, even if a bit late.'

'I've explained about that.'

'Shows she was hanging around before she was killed, I see that.' Yes, it did help a bit after all. One more little fragment of the broken mosaic that was her death and the night when it happened.

'She wasn't on her own,' Foggerty took a deep breath, and her stomach twitched. 'There was someone walking with her.' She had thought a lot about saying this, but it had better be said.

'Well, I never.' Bister swallowed his last gulp of coffee. 'Now it is a pity you didn't tell me that before.'

Sergeant Foggerty shifted uncomfortably but said nothing. She made her excuses.

'And what was this other person like? Anyone you recognised?'

Foggerty shook her head.

'A description, please.' He was pulling out his notebook.

'I couldn't really see. They were moving away fast . . . And like I said, it was raining.'

'Sex? Male or female?'

'They all look the same these days.'

Bister clucked his teeth angrily.

'I didn't know she was going to get killed.'

'Help and no help,' said Bister caustically. He thought for a moment. 'Still, it puts her on the spot with someone who was probably her killer.'

'Might have been,' corrected Sergeant Foggerty.

'I'm going to say yes, it's too much of a coincidence otherwise.'

Margery Foggerty stood up. 'Well, now I've told you.'

Bister shuffled the papers in his notebook. 'Yes, thanks.' Then he gave a brilliant, wicked smile. 'But I already knew.'

'You did?'

'Yes, woman in one of the flats, looking out of a window. Looking for her cat, and she saw them. But I didn't put a lot of weight on it because she's a bit of a fantasist and rings up about once a week, claiming she's seen things. Case of crying wolf, so it seems now. People are telling the truth sometimes. Now with you to back her up, I have to believe her.'

'Right,' said Foggerty, her own voice feeling hollow to her. How many pairs of eyes had seen what? But to her surprise her stomach felt better, she had done the right thing.

'Unluckily she didn't see enough to be much help either. Just two walking figures. But one was definitely Fisher because of the clothes. Like a walking mummy, she said, only black.'

Yes, that was Fisher, as all who knew her could testify.

Later on that day Foggerty saw Bister and Dolly Barstow talking together. They did not look her way but she knew she had been seen. They were probably talking about her and what she had said.

Just a guess, of course, but some guesses seemed to carry their own believable truth with them.

So Barstow would know and would probably tell Charmian Daniels whom gossip reported to be taking a hand. It also reported that she had been offered a plum job locally. Some people did everything right. The woman was even slim and pretty. Maybe too thin, it couldn't be healthy to be too thin. Foggerty took a toffee from her pocket, unwrapped it carefully and started to chew.

I was right to say what I did, though, she decided, but it would have been better if I had done it before I went to Spain.

Somewhat to her own surprise, she slept soundly that night, better, as it happened, than Charmian Daniels, or Dolly Barstow, or Kate Cooper.

And much better than the man who had stood in the bushes across the road and watched Charmian's windows while he smoked his cigar. It was a wet night which did not improve the pleasure of his cigar, but it occupied his hands and his mouth which satisfied him somewhat.

He was a man who sought satisfaction, who hated to be denied. Greedy, if not worse.

On the morning of October 7 when Charmian left her house she was surprised to see a car parked across the street with a man sitting in it. He got out when he saw her and walked across the road.

She recognised him at once. 'Jack.' Jack Cooper, Kate's father and husband of her oldest friend. 'What are you doing here?'

'Waiting for you.' His tone was not pleasant.

'How long have you been here?'

He smelt of whisky and bar-rooms, as if he had been smoked over all night.

'Why didn't you come in?' Still, perhaps as well he hadn't by the look of him.

He ignored the question, but came up closer.

'There is the telephone.' Charmian took a step away.

'This is better said face to face.' He grabbed her arm. 'Not to say shouted.' She tried to shake herself free, but he hung on. 'Don't move away.'

'Keep your voice down.' She looked at the house next door. Of course, the window curtains twitched.

'I'm angry with you. Very very angry. I've never liked you.'

'That's not true, we've got on well enough.'

'I put up with you. But you're an arrogant interfering bitch.'

'And you're a bastard. You're drunk, Jack,' said Charmian with weary tolerance. She'd seen Jack in this state before. They all had.

'How dare you put my wife against me, and my daughter?'

'Oh, rubbish.'

'Rubbish, is it? Letting Kate and Annie think I made a pass at that other bitch, Sergeant Dolly Barstow, CID.'

'I expect you did, Jack, you do, you know.'

'Don't you patronise me.'

'But as it happens it wasn't me. It was Nella Fisher. Who is now dead. What about that, Jack?'

There was a moment of silence. Just for a second, she thought he would hit her.

He took a step back. 'I'll get you for that. You don't understand men. You don't know how a man's mind works. I'll show you.'

He turned back towards the car.

'You shouldn't be driving in your state,' she called out.

He got into the car and turned in her direction. She thought he would drive straight at her, then he reversed sharply, swung the car round, and drove off very fast.

Charmian took a deep breath. Just for a moment, Jack had looked like murder.

Fury swept over her. 'I'll be round to see you, Jack,' she called. 'Damn you.'

She had known Jack for years, sometimes been angry with him for his behaviour, sometimes pitied him because Annie could be quite a handful, often found him amusing. He was a witty man even in his cups. Never, ever had she felt frightened of him.

Now, for the first time, she felt the threat of personal violence.

## CHAPTER SEVEN

## *Saturday, October 7 to Monday October 9*

Two days passed, during which nothing much seemed to happen in the investigation, or nothing that came to Charmian's ears. She knew that the routine enquiries would be proceeding. The Major Incident Room in River Walk would be in full operation, but you could not expect developments all the time. They had come to one of those patches, and it happens in all investigations, when everything goes quiet. With luck, it would burst into life again and hurry forward. Or, if not luck, then patient hard work will often do the trick. Sometimes, of course, nothing does, and that case remains open. The file is never closed on a murder investigation.

Charmian had two busy days in London, during which the Nella Fisher case was always at the back of her mind as she attended to administrative duties, wrote letters and memoranda and chaired two committees.

She had calmed down in her anger with Jack Cooper, but not forgiven him or forgotten him. She would deal with him. Her sense of personal danger had faded somewhat while not quite going away. But you couldn't think of Jack as a killer, not Jack whose wedding you had attended (and he had been pretty hungover at that too), and whose hand you had held while his child was born, whom you had protected once or twice from the onslaughts of an angry Annie. He had not been around again, or she didn't think so, but yet she had had the feeling as she parked the car or opened the window for the cat at night that there was someone outside.

She had her own private and personal problems too. They could be summarised under hair, Humphrey, and clothes. She chose to bracket her problems under these headings and in this order (which said something in itself), but what she was really confronting was a career problem. A life-style problem. If she took the job on offer, and if, as she might, she married Humphrey, what sort of a life would she have, what sort of a woman would she be? Life did shape you so, no use pretending otherwise. So often, you were not a free agent, not even in charge.

This hiatus was a time to be accepted as part of the process, and Charmian accepted it. Went on with her life, visited her hairdresser, looked at some new clothes, did not buy any, was telephoned by Humphrey who, it turned out, was no longer in Geneva but in Bonn, and was not home to receive his call. Same old work pattern, though. She also wrote two letters about the new position she had been offered: one accepting, one refusing. She had till the end of the month to decide. She weighed herself, down again, another pound gone. Do you do something about it, she asked herself, or be grateful? Didn't the Duchess of Windsor say that no woman can be too thin? Simply not true.

During this time, Sergeant Dolly Barstow and Kate Cooper were elusive. Charmian felt convinced that Dolly was still holding something back.

Kate was around, that was about all one could say. She had come in over the weekend with a book to lend to Charmian about the French Revolution that she thought her godmother ought to read (trust Kate to admire Robespierre); in addition she brought her a cake from a famous patisserie, but would not stay to eat it. 'You need to eat it up though, every calorific slice. Promise?' Then she reported that she thought the police still had an eye on her, but of how she really felt inside, she said nothing. Charmian, watching her, was biding her time.

It was stormy weather, with strong wet winds. Walking home from the railway station by the River Thames, Charmian saw how branches of trees had been tossed into the water by the gale of the night before. The currents were pulling the logs together in loose swirling masses as they passed down the river. She stood looking at them, thinking that was how it was at the moment in

72

the Nella Fisher case, with a lot of different elements jostling for place and getting in each other's way.

Then the log jam broke: Dolly Barstow sent her the file on Nella's last days. She delivered it by hand, pushing it through Charmian's letterbox in the late afternoon of October 9, with a note. Her note said: For your information.

Only Muff the cat was at home to receive it at the time and she sat on it thoughtfully with muddy paws. Then, growing bored, she pretended it was something she had caught, chewing at the corners of the envelope with her sharp little teeth, then turning round and tearing at it with her back paws.

Charmian rescued the mauled packet when she came in and bore it into the kitchen where she studied it over a chicken sandwich, followed by a slice of the chocolate and almond cake from Maison Blanc and a cup of coffee. Muff had long since departed to sleep off her maraudings. Paper must be filling, Charmian thought.

When she had read it, for no reason whatever that she could identify, but which must be there under the surface, she rang up her doctor and made an appointment for the next day.

'You love worrying,' she told herself vengefully. Lumps and bumps, what did they amount to?

She consulted her diary and made a few telephone calls; her London appointments for the next day could be rearranged. Then she tossed up whether she should go to Cheasey to see the family of Nella Fisher, all those Fishers, Seamans and Rivers and Waters who had been so reluctant to attend the girl's funeral, or go to see Jack and Annie Cooper. Jack on his own for preference, but that might be hard to achieve.

Heads for Cheasey, tails for Jack and Annie.

The coin fell face up.

She was going to Cheasey. It was what she wanted anyway.

Cheasey was an easy drive along the Slough road, the traffic was heavy but slow-moving, all you needed was patience. Not the quality that Charmian was strongest in, but today she felt strong and quiet. She had the radio on and a Beethoven quartet was being played. No self-pity in that man.

Up to the Slough-Cheasey roundabout, then behind a huge

lorry heading for the motorway and leaving the road before her clear. Then a drive through suburban streets with factories and workshops on either side. Then she was through the industrial area into row upon row of small houses, with here and there a tall block of dwellings where the inhabitants must feel like cave-dwellers.

A few stunted trees hung on at irregular intervals, dusty and depressed, like a parade of forgotten soldiers. Cars lined the kerbs on either side so that driving down the narrow path between needed care. A public house, The Grey Man, with a large car park, gave Charmian somewhere to stop while she looked at a road map.

Yes, she was close to the house where one enclave of the Fisher family lived. Knowing from Dolly Barstow what a strange and inchoate group they were, with family members moving around from house to house as it suited them, she had to hope that 12 Duke Road was where Nella Fisher had called home.

She thought she knew the road. At one time, and not so long ago, when she had been a part-time student at the University in Uxbridge, writing a thesis on Women in Crime, she had driven these streets often as she sought out criminous women willing to be interviewed. Cheasey had provided a rich field. Interestingly, no member of the Fisher clan had come forward to be questioned, although many could be nominated, with one or two she had heard tell worthy of the title 'Woman Criminal of the Year'.

She locked the car – you locked everything in Cheasey, nailed it down if possible or when you came back it was gone – and went into The Grey Man for a glass of dry sherry and a little prospecting of the landscape. She seemed to recall that the place had formerly been called The Packhorse Inn which seemed to suggest a change of ownership.

A change of policy also, perhaps? She remembered it as a place of darkness and quiet; now it was painted, too well lit and noisy with music. The woman behind the bar had pretty red hair teased into a wildness, a kind of froth, and wore earrings that dangled brightly towards her waist. She had strong mauve, blue and turquoise shadows painted above her eyes into which baby-blue contact lenses had been inserted so that her gaze was as bright and lucid as a fish. She had overdone it, but Cheasey pushed you to extremes.

The bright eyes had no difficulty in assessing Charmian, deciding what she was, and possibly even estimating her rank. Or she may just have come across Charmian in the past.

She pushed the sherry across the bar without comment.

'I'm looking for Duke Street. I believe it's around here somewhere.'

The blue eyes, behind which paler eyes lurked, became vague. 'Dunno,' she said. 'Duke, you say? There's a Queen street.'

'Duke,' said Charmian firmly.

'Prince Albert road?'

'You don't know Duke Street?'

'Looking for a friend?'

'Not exactly,' said Charmian.

The blue eyes, which could not cloud because of their constituent parts, had begun to water a little so that the woman had to pat them with a tissue. The rainbow of eye shadows began to run. 'Bert,' she called over her shoulder. 'Do we know where Duke Street is?'

A man appeared from the back, a plump man in a striped shirt with a bow-tie. He looked like an out-of-work actor, but a lot of men had that look these days. 'Duke Street? Round the corner somewhere, isn't it?'

'Do you know anyone who lives there? Mrs Fisher?'

'Don't think so. Fisher? We don't do we, Ginny?'

Ginny did not answer, she was repairing her eye makeup. 'These bloody lenses,' she muttered. 'Well, I wouldn't. I hardly know anyone round here if they don't drink here.'

'Silly question,' said Charmian, taking her sherry away to a seat in the window.

She sipped her drink, pretending to study a map, while making a discreet survey of the room.

She was immediately aware that she was the object of scrutiny herself. The room had filled even in the short time since she had arrived. A group of men sitting in one corner, were talking away loudly; they were also watching her in a wall mirror. A man in the next window recess was reading a newspaper and keeping an eye on her.

Ginny and Bert were maintaining a covert watch too.

Well, well, it began to look as if she might have walked into the very pub in which Nella had worked, and in which Dolly Barstow had taken a drink. She could go up to the bar and question Ginny and Bert, but they seemed a pair of obstinate non-answerers. Not subtle but dogged.

It was more than possible too that Nella, who seemed to have a different name for every place, had not called herself Fisher. Possibly not even Nella. But Bert and Ginny, who looked as though nothing got past them, would certainly know who she was.

But they were not going to admit it, they did not want to talk about it. They were very wary in this place. This was surprising in itself because people like Bert and Ginny were usually anxious to keep in well with the police.

Depended on who used their bar, of course, and for what purpose.

While still studying her map and apparently writing a few notes, she observed the faces of the men. No one she knew, but they fell into a type. Rough men trying to look respectable, men on the edge of the law. One or two of them had probably done time. She would take an oath on it. That one with the dark spectacles and pale face and thick hands, that one across the room with his newspaper. She could bet he knew his way around Fitcham Prison.

They all had an air of watching and waiting. Waiting for someone? Well, they hadn't been waiting for her. She was an unexpected and, she would swear, an unwelcome arrival.

As she finished her sherry and made to go, the door swung open to admit a man. He was tall, well built, with a large head. A crop of wiry brown curls, a tanned skin and a broken nose. He was wearing a well-cut blue blazer with a crest on the pocket and brass buttons. A clean white shirt of which the cuffs could just be seen at his wrist. He had large but nicely manicured hands with a ring on his little finger.

Charmian knew his face. They had met, but not socially. A man whose face had known many a mug shot. He had a record and a place in the history of crime.

She fumbled for his name. Jake something. Her memory

quickly provided a few facts. Jake Henley, alias Joe Howard, and sometimes Jo Headlam. He stuck to the same initials, because he was a natty dresser who liked to have his clothes initialled.

Porn, and drugs, were his speciality, although he was reputed to be willing to try anything in which he would not actually get his own hands dirty.

He had been inside, but never for as long as he deserved. No one regretted it more than Charmian who had tried hard to put him there once herself. The day of the trial had been the day that the photograph stuck on Nella's wall had been taken. Coincidence? She hated coincidences.

The audience in The Grey Man was quiet. This was the man for whom they had been waiting.

Jake walked quietly to the bar, collected his drink and took it to a solitary seat by the fire. Perhaps it had been left vacant for him. He acted as if it was his by right. There was a comfortable chair next to it, but no one moved to take it. You had to be invited.

Assembling her thoughts, Charmian remembered that Jake Henley had managed to stay in the background of the porn case she had investigated and brought to court. A group of people, women as well as men, more's the pity, had gone to prison for a lot longer than he had. Heavy fines had been imposed. I must have put a spoke in quite a few lives, she thought. Perhaps in that man's.

Charmian got up, picked up her bag and started to walk towards the door. Henley looked up and stared at her. Their eyes met.

That man hates me, Charmian thought. It hit her hard. What a lot of male hostility I seem to be stirring up lately. More than usual, and there had always been a bit of it around her. She was used to provoking rough brushes with the male ego, as every successful woman must. But she could ignore those: they were all in the way of business.

But she could not ignore this display of feeling, it was altogether more personal.

No one else moved, and she walked across to her car, feeling a tingling down her spine. Yes, she was scared. Better to admit it.

She started the car while she savoured the thought it had been in The Grey Man that Dolly Barstow had seen the bent copper meeting the porn king. It had a rich flavour, that thought.

This was where Roger, so-called, had met Jake Henley, so-called.

If that was the man who had it in for Dolly Barstow, then Dolly was in trouble indeed.

Any woman would be.

Her thoughts took their own unprompted course as she turned the car towards Duke Street.

Odd that man coming into The Grey Man just when she was there. Luck or unluck, depending on how you felt about it.

She waited for the traffic lights to change. Perhaps it wasn't luck at all. Perhaps he had come because he knew she was there. A telephone call from Bert or Ginny as they darted in and out would have done it.

In a way, she preferred that possibility, with her inbuilt, police dislike of coincidences. But it introduced other elements that would need thinking about. Like, why would he want to bother? And what lay behind his dislike of her?

Perhaps he just disliked all policewomen on principle.

The lights changed to green and she moved off.

Cheasey was much as she remembered it. The rows of houses with their small gardens, some cared for, even cherished, others used as a dumping ground for bits of old cars and bikes. One front garden had an ambulance parked in it and another parked outside. Last time she had come this way it had been old fire engines the house-owner had collected. Obviously he had now diversified into ambulances.

She was glad to see that particular garden, it had been a landmark in her memory. It was good to see people behaving the way they always had.

Past the old ambulances, a turn to the left, and she was in Duke Street. This too was unchanged, part of a large housing estate built by the local authority after the last war. Duke Street was a long vista of small semi-detached houses with a high-rise block of dwellings at the end, sealing it off, making a dead end.

Charmian drove along slowly, checking the numbers as she

did so. The Fishers lived about halfway along Duke Street. Two cars were parked at the kerb outside, each having the hangdog, dejected air of a vehicle that has not been moved for weeks and very possibly can no longer be driven. The tyres had an ominously flat look to them. But beyond them were a couple of smarter, newer cars that were too good for Duke Street.

She found an empty space, parked her own car, locked it with care, and walked back, passing the new cars and the old, automatically observing as she did so, and from old habit, that the licence on each window of the two old cars was well out of date.

The Fisher front garden was average in disorder for the street, possibly even a fraction tidier than its neighbour on the right, because someone had once cut the little patch of grass and planted a few shrubs. True, a family of cats seemed to be living amongst them in wooden boxes but the creatures looked well fed.

She rang the bell, but it made no sound, so she banged on the door. Then she waited. She was pretty certain someone was observing her from behind the curtain of an upstairs window, but she pretended not to notice. Cautious people, the Fishers, wouldn't do to frighten them. Not more than was necessary, anyway.

Presently she heard footsteps approaching. The door opened, but was kept on a chain so that all she saw was a woman's face. Middle-aged, curly blonde hair, but not natural because you could see a rim of dark near the scalp, eyes with the rings of colour that seemed so fashionable in Cheasey and an unwelcoming expression in the mouth.

'Mrs Fisher?'

'No.'

'Do you know where I could find her then? Nella Fisher's mother.' Charmian said quickly: 'That's you, isn't it? You are Mrs Fisher?'

'I'm Rivers now. I was Fisher when I had her.' It was said without much expression. Fisher yesterday, Rivers today, Seaman tomorrow.

'Chief Superintendent Charmian Daniels.' Charmian showed her credentials.

'I know you.' Mrs River's voice, husky from smoking and much shouting up and down the pavements of Cheasey since childhood, gave nothing away. 'What do you want?'

'I want to talk about Nella. I'd like to know about her.' And because I am anxious about a beloved goddaughter. 'May I come in?'

After a pause, Mrs Rivers opened the door. 'All right. I'm busy, mind.'

As she went in, Charmian said: 'Are those cars parked out there yours?'

'Might be.' She sounded indifferent.

'And those cats? Are they yours too? Do they live out there?'

'They've got fleas,' said Mrs Rivers, showing sudden feeling. 'Quick, don't let that one get in.' A large black animal had made a speedy dash for the door and was squeezing past.

The cat fled down the passage. Mrs Rivers shrugged. 'Damned animal.' She led the way to the sitting room at the back of the house. Another woman was sitting at a table there, as if waiting. She did not rise, or smile, or speak. Or not to Charmian. To Mrs Rivers, she said: 'Shall I put the kettle on, Freda?'

'Don't bother, Ju.' Freda sat at the table herself, and motioned to Charmian. 'She won't be staying long. Wants to talk about Nella.'

The cat had got into the room, and was sitting on the windowill, with its tail lashing back and forth.

'That damned Timmy's back in again,' said Ju, and gave an absent-minded scratch.

Why did Charmian have the feeling that there were other people in the house? She had the notion that, although there were just these two women in the sitting room, off-stage somewhere, perhaps upstairs or in another room, was a masculine presence. The women had been pushed into the front, the men hid in the background.

'I can't tell you much about her. She didn't keep in touch, our Nella. Pushed off. Did her own thing. That's what she said.'

'Came back,' said Ju.

'Well, that's true. On and off.'

'Weren't you worried about her?'

'She could look after herself.'

Manifestly untrue, Charmian thought.

'She had a nice little job at one time, working for Mr Dick in Merrywick at the Keyright Bureau. I got her that work. Used to clean for his mother till she died. I got Nella in there, but she got too big for her boots, wanted to be a secretary or get a degree. I let her get on with it. I lost touch then. Couldn't keep up.'

'You did see her, though,' Ju reminded her. 'She came back.'

'When?' asked Charmian, keeping a wary eye on the flea-ridden Timmy.

'Just before she went away.'

'Went away where?'

'Died.' It was a bleak statement.

'Why did she come then?' asked Charmian.

'I dunno. She didn't say. Just came. I shall miss her, though.'

'Yes, I'm sorry,' said Charmian.

'You hardly ever saw her,' said Ju, who seemed to enjoy dropping her ironic little comments into the pool.

'You can miss someone even if you don't see them. I knew she was there.'

Charmian tried again. She had to get something out of this woman, she felt she was holding back. 'You talked, though? You didn't sit in silence. What did she say?'

'She told us she was going to die.'

Charmian felt the shock and surprise.

'I reckon that was why she came.'

Charmian did not know what to say. She said nothing, and scratched her leg.

'So when she did, we thought she had killed herself.'

Again deep in her state of shock, Charmian said: 'But she didn't.'

'So we found out.'

'But what made you think she would want to kill herself?'

There was silence in the room. Outside a child was crying and someone was trying to start a car.

Freda gave Charmian a look of ironic amusement. 'You don't know much, do you?'

'Obviously not enough.'

'She had it.'

'Had what?'

Freda raised her eyebrows, then leaned forward and whispered in Charmian's ear.

Nella had been HIV positive. She had told her mother. As she listened, Charmian thought she heard feet passing quietly down the stairs.

'Is that why you didn't come to the funeral?'

'Yes. Leave it there, we thought. She told us not to come and we didn't. "Don't watch me being buried," she said. "I wouldn't fancy it." So we did what she said. Kept out.'

'Thanks for explaining,' said Charmian. 'I'll let myself out, shall I?'

The cat came with her, giving a quick scratch as he passed though the door, following her down the street and making a good attempt to get into the car with her, so that she had to make haste.

She sat in her car for a little while, getting her breath back. She noticed that the new cars had gone, while the old remained, as dusty and immovable as ever.

A sequence of events was unfolding itself before her inward eyes. Nella had gone to give blood. As a consequence of this act, she had learned that she was infected.

Desperate, either for money to ease her plight, she had gone to see Kate and Dolly.

She had used threats, and offered a dangerous story to sell. And as a consequence of that, someone had killed her.

Perhaps Nella had also been looking for a quick death.

Driving back to Windsor, she felt a distinct and wandering itch up and down her leg.

That damned Timmy.

When Charmian got home she had a very hot bath, in which she hoped that any Cheasey fleas were floating. She would have bathed anyway, somehow Cheasey needed washing off you.

The great majority of the inhabitants of Cheasey neither knew her nor cared about her, but that little group connected with Nella both knew her and disliked her.

She had at least one enemy there: Jake Henley in The Grey Man, and she felt the force of his dislike. Hate, even.

She avoided the bathroom scales as she dressed; she had

made her appointment with the doctor and that was that. But she felt a sudden chill as if her inside was being searched with cold, sterile steel.

She sat down and rested her head on her hands. In her profession you were allowed to be a woman, but not too female. But whatever it meant to be a woman, she suddenly felt very female indeed.

On her dressing table were the two tickets for a Mozart concert which Humphrey had sent. 'I'd hoped we could go together,' he had written. 'But it's not to be. I hope you will use them.'

She'd go. She dressed carefully, and booked herself a table in the French restaurant near to the concert hall in Waterloo Street.

After all, Humphrey had sent her flowers. There was a box on her doorstep. Flowers to wear? She started to open it.

No, wait a minute, not flowers. Inside was a bottle. An unpleasant-looking bottle. Small, dark, and with a handwritten label. VITRIOL, it said.

A faint smell of cigar smoke seemed to cling to the paper. Or was that just her imagination?

When she examined it carefully, with gloved hands, she was convinced that the liquid was not vitriol. On a closer scrutiny it did not have the right smell or look. Of course, it would have to be checked professionally, but she was convinced it was a fake.

No joke though. The threat was there. She felt the reality of it. No acid thrown at her this time, but some time soon? That was what the bottle was saying. Watch it, Charmian Daniels, you are an object of my hate.

She went to the concert, but she did not enjoy it.

# CHAPTER EIGHT

## *Tuesday, October 10, to Wednesday, October 11*

Dolly, Dolly, Nella, Nella, Kate, Kate, the names ran through her mind like a song with one strong melody. It even got into the concert, weaving in and out of the concerto, each different theme sounding: AIDS, Nella, Kate, Dolly, Jack's gun.

But in the end Mozart was triumphant, consoling and soothing to the spirit, wiping out the names and horrors so that Charmian slept well, a peaceful cat bedding down beside her. She ate her breakfast toast while she made a list of what she needed to do that day.

First thing, she put the vitriol in a plastic bag, ready to be collected. Then she informed both the local police and her own Metropolitan unit about the implied threat of the vitriol. She was pretty sure, by that time, it was not vitriol.

An officer from the Datchet Road station was despatched to interview her at home.

On the telephone, The Met Unit briefed her on the security measures she should be taking herself. Checking her car, seeing the house was properly locked up, treating packages with suspicion. All things she knew.

'Again,' the London man said with some emphasis. 'Told you this before. Don't think you take it seriously.' Although the speaker was much junior in rank to Charmian, his work was of so important and sensitive a nature that he took himself very seriously indeed.

'Oh I do,' said Charmian.

'Good. I'll liaise with the Windsor unit, Eddie Vander is

the local man, I've worked with him before. Might be the Henley chap doing it but one can't count on it. Good that you recognised him. Or it could be a villain from up here that's got it in for you. More likely, I'd say. But we'll see.' He was pretty confident of his ability to find her frightener, it was his business to be reassuring.

Dolly was next on her list. Charmian felt a certain urgency about this, because she wanted to get on to Kate herself and Dolly, who was coming to be a kind of obstacle, had to be cleared out of the way first.

Pretty, hard-working, ambitious Dolly was usually a support. Not this time, however. Something was getting in the way.

The visit to the unlovely suburb of Cheasey had added extra shading to her picture of Nella Fisher, provided a motive for the girl's desperation, for her feeling that she must get money.

It had even fleshed out her story of the threatening man, possibly given him a face. The man called Jake Henley.

Maybe also put a name on the killer. It could be Henley himself. Or, as Dolly Barstow seemed to believe, the bent policeman with whom he was supposed to be in contact.

It was time to put Inspector Elman and Sergeant Bister in the picture so that they could dig deep into the background of Jake Henley and flush up evidence about this corrupt relationship.

But first things first. Dolly Barstow seemed to know more than she was telling and had better part with this information.

Dolly heard her out on the phone, picked up all the tension and reservations, and said briefly that she'd be over soon. Soon as she could polish off what was on her desk. Charmian might be able to call the tune, rearrange her work, but such pleasures of seniority were not for Sergeant Barstow.

A difficult new case had come in: the theft of some major and important jewellery from an illustrious house in the Great Park that should be free from such depredations. Dolly had interviewed the chief suspect and was writing up her notes. She would not continue on the case, it was too tricky, too important, too secret. A bloke was coming down from London to take over. Meanwhile, she must record her first impression, even if it meant keeping Charmian waiting. It was easy for her, Dolly thought a touch enviously, since she was top of her particular tree.

As a matter of fact, Charmian had not found it easy. A little prevarication had been necessary on the telephone. A committee could be missed, she was not in the chair, an appointment put off, letters and memos dictated over the telephone, but it wasn't something to be done too often.

She had enough worldliness to do it without offering an explanation. She would have done so once, entangled herself in a variety of excuses, but not now. Now she just got on with what seemed right and let people make what they liked of it.

Underneath, she was aware that a resolution was forming about the new position on offer: she must be going to accept. Silently she was moving away from the London end and repositioning herself.

She dressed carefully in a thin Italian jersey suit made in the subtle yet vivid colours which Missoni used. She dressed well now and she knew it. Books might furnish a room, but clothes did prop up a woman.

Dolly arrived unexpectedly soon.'Can't stay long.'

'Work piling up?' Should she tell her about the vitriol? No, later.

'That, too. Someone has nicked the Crown Jewels. No, not really, but nearly as good as,' said Dolly, 'but my real problem is my car has packed up and George Rewley gave me a lift, but he's in a hurry. On his way to an interview. He'll be back in about an hour.' She looked at Charmian. 'So?'

'I've been out to Cheasey. Inspecting where Nella lived.'

'You didn't take George?'

'No.' Charmian poured them both some coffee. She didn't have to explain herself to George Rewley. Although he might have been useful.

'George says Cheasey is a thieves' kitchen.'

So they were back to George, were they, relationship warming up again? Kate's own fault if she'd lost George who was so well worth keeping.

'He's right. And I think it might be as well to send a man there to have a look at the cars parked along the kerb outside the Fishers' house. It's Rivers now, by the way. Mrs Rivers.'

'You think the cars are stolen?'

'Some of them, not others.' The battered ones hadn't looked the sort of car anyone would want to steal; no market for them, not without a bit of work on them which none of the Rivers-Fisher clan seemed likely to do. 'But there's something odd about them.'

She didn't call me here just to tell me that, decided Dolly. 'I'll see to it. Is that what you wanted me for?'

'No, and you know it. I can read your face, Dolly. George Rewley isn't the only one to be able to read body signals. I studied the notes on Nella Fisher's last days. Thank you for getting them to me. She was certainly on the move.'

'Restless,' said Dolly.

'She had something on her mind. And now we know what it probably was.'

'The positive blood test? HIV positive. Poor kid.'

'I agree. She was desperate. I think that's why she wanted money. To get away, to get out, or just to make her life more tolerable. She could see what was coming and didn't like it. She may even have hoped somehow she would be killed. Quicker, easier.'

'She could have been tempting someone to kill her. Consciously or unconsciously. I think I can understand that.'

'She more or less told her mother that. She was going to die, she said to her mother.'

'As, one way or another, she was.'

'They thought of suicide.'

'They knew about the blood test?'

'I think that's why they didn't come to the funeral.'

'Probably thought they'd catch something,' said Dolly sourly.

'No, I don't rate them as bad as that. I think it was a sign of their distress. In their way I think they loved Nella. Not in everyone's way, but I wouldn't call Mrs Rivers completely unfeeling.' Not a lot of evidence one way or another, but Charmian had that conviction. She had seen something in Mrs Rivers's eyes of distress and grief. Kindness too. After all, even the flea-ridden cats were still there, housed and fed.

She went on: 'When I was in Cheasey, I dropped in at a pub called The Grey Man.'

'Ah,' said Dolly.

'Yes, you kept something from me there, didn't you, Dolly?'

Dolly gave a small shrug.

'And I've been asking myself why.'

'I was thinking things over,' said Dolly.

'I sat in that bar and I didn't like the feel of it at all. All eyes on me. Not a nice place. Then a man called Jake Henley came in. I don't know if that is the name he is using now, but he used it once. He has a record for porn dealing, drugs, the lot. Not a nice man. I think you've sat in that bar, Dolly, and that it was where Roger met his contact, and that Henley was that contact.'

'Yes,' said Dolly, with a sigh. 'That's where they met. Nella Fisher worked there for a bit. I think that's where she picked up her tale of the threats. If she didn't make it up just to get funds.'

'I don't think she made anything up,' said Charmian quietly. 'Although she may have got things wrong. Do you think Henley killed Nella?'

'I think he might have done,' said Dolly. 'But I cannot be quite sure. No proof. But he's got the touch.'

Dolly's face looked troubled. She put her coffee cup down unsteadily so that the coffee spilled on the table. She mopped at it with a tissue, not meeting Charmian's eyes.

'But it could have been Roger. Roger was there when Nella died. I saw Roger.' The words came out slowly as if she did not want to utter them.

Look at me, Dolly, thought Charmian, but did not say so aloud. 'Yes, so I remember you saying.'

'And then, she put herself on the spot with a story about seeing someone walking with Nella. Admitted it. To me, that was a confession.'

Charmian was startled. 'What's that you said?'

'Yes, her. She. WPS Margery Foggerty. Roger is a woman. You never thought of that, did you?'

Over coffee, they talked. The question was, why had Roger come forward with the story of seeing a figure walking with Nella?

'I think she believed someone might have seen her from a window and she'd better get her story in first.'

So the killer of Nella could be, they reasoned, Sergeant Foggerty herself. Dolly seemed to think it was likely, but proof was another thing.

Charmian considered. She didn't like it.

'Why didn't you tell me all this before?'

'Foggerty saved my life once. Early in my career, knocked over a chap whom I was trying to question and who came at me with an axe. She was brave and quick. I owed her.'

Charmian shook her head. Police loyalty, man to man, and now woman to woman. It was a good thing, but it could go too far.

The front-door bell rang. Loudly, twice. Charmian went to answer it. There on the doorstep was a messenger from Security. 'Parcel to collect.'

She handed over the packet containing the bottle of vitriol. The poisoned message, the threat that she didn't want to admit to worrying about. Silly stuff, no need to bother over it, that was how she ought to feel but could not.

'Sign, please.' He held out a form. Everything in Security was signed and recorded, sometimes in triplicate. 'And a note from Sergeant Vander, ma'am.'

It was a polite message from Eddie Vander, whom she knew very slightly, asking for a meeting.

Dolly looked up curiously.

'Someone left a bottle of vitriol on my doorstep last night.'

'What?'

'Well, I suspect it's not vitriol, but the threat is there. I'm meant to be frightened.'

I am not frightened, she said to herself. Not yet.

'I don't know if it has any connection with Nella Fisher's murder, but it might be connected with my visit to Cheasey. They didn't like me there. Warning me off might seem a good idea.'

Dolly stood up. 'I'll get to work on Foggerty. I shall have to go through channels. I'll report what I saw. But I think it's not going to be an enjoyable time.' A faint note of protest was sounded there.

'No.' Did she expect it to be, thought Charmian with a touch of irritation. Why did both Dolly and Kate have this conviction that somehow, for them, all paths would be cleared? 'And Jake? What about him?'

'Well, it will all be in the report, but in addition, I'll talk to Elman. Better him than Bister.' Although he would have to be faced as well, and she could see that she would have to go all the way up to Chief Inspector Father, and fatherly he probably would not be. Life was not going to be agreeable. The career of Sergeant Dolly Barstow had taken a step backward. 'There will be an enquiry. Dirty linen coming out to be washed. Everyone will hate that and a bit of nastiness will wash off on us all.'

'Yes, a grubby business.'

'I dropped myself in it. I should have spoken about Foggerty ages ago.' No self-pity but still a bit of a surprise that life should be hard for such as Sergeant Dolly Barstow.

'Yes, you should.' She'll learn, Charmian thought. Sympathy was one thing, but overlooking an error of judgement, even if you understood it, was another. 'Go on,' she said to Dolly. 'Go off and set the machine in motion.'

That put Kate Cooper in the clear, she thought.

'It's got a sharp cutting edge, that machine,' said Dolly wryly. Muff rubbed against her legs and she bent down to pat the hard little head. 'I can always retire and keep a cat farm.'

But it was not all right, Charmian thought. Foggerty might have killed Nella Fisher, but there was still this story of the threats. Had it been Foggerty and Jake planning to damage Dolly, who had seen them together?

But what about Kate's story that Nella had talked about Jack? And Kate's gun?

It was time she looked in at the Incident Room in River Walk and spoke to Bister, and Fred Elman if he was there. Perhaps they would let her borrow Rewley again. In fact, they would probably insist on it. Let Chief Superintendent Charmian Daniels wander around on her own? Never.

She watched Dolly Barstow drive off with George. While she herself decided what to do next.

As if on cue the telephone rang as Dolly left. It was Kate.

'Oh Kate, I want to talk to you.' Question you, she meant,

hardly bothering to disguise her intention. There were times, and this was one of them, when her police training showed through more than it should. But it was part of her now, built into her, Charmian Daniels, woman police officer, successful and influential. Not everyone liked that side of her, she didn't always like it herself.

'I'm glad you're there. I thought you might be in London.'

'I shall be later in the day.' This was true, she had a late appointment in London. 'Where are you, Kate?'

'I'm at Mother's. Will you come over?'

Jack and Annie Cooper lived in Wellington Yard which was off Peascod Street, a cobbled area of small shops, dwelling places, and the studio and art gallery belonging to Annie. Charmian had lived there once herself as Annie's lodger when she was doing a research degree at the university. It had been a happy time in her life, her first break into the bigger, metropolitan world. From then on, her career had gone up and up. Yes, she liked Wellington Yard and had enjoyed her stay with Annie, quarrelling occasionally as old friends can without breaking the link.

But Jack was different. She was afraid he disliked her now, for reasons she could not quite grasp. Just for being herself probably, the most dangerous reason of all.

'Anything wrong?' she asked Kate. More than usual, she meant, since Jack and Annie fought and were reconciled all the time. Sometimes Jack left home, sometimes Annie took off for Paris or Rome or New York, returning usually in an excellent temper and having forgotten what the quarrel was all about. No wonder Kate was so often on the wing. Like mother like daughter.

'Yes. Dad's gone off. No, really missing this time. Not in any of his usual haunts. I've checked.' When Jack departed in a temper, as a rule he did not go far since he had none of the financial resources of his wife and daughter. Jack did not sponge on the family money. For his own personal use he had only the money he earned. This was small and irregular in amount. 'He's been in a raging foul mood lately. Hating us all.'

'I know.'

'Has he been along to shout at you?'

'Yes.'

'I thought he might have. He was drunk, of course.' Often Jack was able to drink and not show the effects. If anything, it made him a more pleasant companion, and in many ways he was an enjoyable person to be with. Indeed, it was hard to dislike Jack even when he was at his wildest. Or so it had always been in the past. 'It's the murder. He knows all the stories that are going round and he's frightened.'

'He ought to be frightened for you.'

'That too,' said Kate sadly. 'Although he doesn't admit it. He does love me, you know. Annie too. They love each other when they let go.'

'You don't have to tell me. I know that.'

Wellington Yard was an attractive place to live now, although it had not always been so. Had it once been an old builder's yard or belonged to a brewery? The locals told different stories. Annie, who was rich, had started with a gallery and an apartment above it, but she now owned the premises next door where she kept a self-contained flat for guests and a large studio. Kate, the apprentice architect, had designed the interior so that it was full of large, white, empty spaces with a cantilevered staircase. The walls were hung with the contemporary art that Annie collected and dealt in.

Charmian drove in and parked outside Annie's. Two large bay trees in red tubs marked the front door. The colour of the tubs changed with Annie's mood; she went out and slapped the paint on herself. They had been red for some weeks now.

Red was a bad sign and meant anger in the home.

Kate's face was peering through the glass panels of the door: that was another bad sign.

She opened the door at once. 'Thank goodness.'

'Where's your mother?'

'Upstairs breaking crockery.' Kate started to lead the way through to the lift which Annie had installed in a flamboyant gesture, saying it was for her old age. The Cooper family did go on to a great age: Annie's mother was still alive and living in Florence.

'Wait a minute.' Charmian held Kate back. 'I want to talk before we go up.'

From above, Annie called hoarsely, as if she had been shouting: 'Char? Come on up.'

92

'Coming. Just taking my coat off.'

She turned to Kate. 'About the gun, Kate. It wasn't your gun, was it?'

'No.'

'Good. I thought not. You never got a gun in India. You've never had a gun for self-protection or anything.'

'No,' Kate gave a small smile. 'I'm a karate black belt. Well, that's not true. But I did take a course. I prefer self-help to guns.'

This was the authentic Kate talking.

'So, whose gun? Don't tell me, I can guess. It belonged to Jack.'

'Yes, it was his gun.'

'And why did you take it? Don't tell me again, let me guess. Because he'd been shouting his mouth off about me and Dolly and anyone he was angry with at the moment. Including probably the Pope and the Prince of Wales.'

'Yes,' Kate gave a relieved grin. 'Especially the Prince of Wales. You are taking it well.'

'I'm taking it well because there is another hot suspect for killing Nella Fisher. But don't think you are off the hook. Nor Jack.'

Charmian got into the lift and pressed the button. It shot up. Things always moved with speed in Annie Cooper's house.

'That coat took a bloody long time to get off,' called Annie as the lift rose.

The next half-hour was not an easy one, but Charmian succeeded in calming Annie. They were old friends and could manage each other. This time it took some soothing words of authority.

'I'll see that there's a discreet search made for Jack, but I can't promise anything.'

Annie accepted this and calmed down. Charmian could see she was now more frightened about Jack's disappearance than angry. 'He hasn't got any money,' she kept saying. 'How will he manage?'

'Lack of money has never stopped Jack before,' Charmian reminded her.

'I should have been more generous to him,' mourned Annie.

'Remember that when he comes back,' said Charmian.

She let Kate see her to the car. 'Kate, did your father have more than one gun?'

Kate did not like the question but she answered it. 'I think so. One of his pub pals had a small collection and Jack bought them off him when he was short of cash.'

'With ammunition too, I take it?'

'I expect so, but Dad knew where to get some, anyway. Another drinking pal keeps a gun shop.'

'And no licence, I suppose?'

Kate shook her head. No need to answer that one. Jack was a permanently unlicensed person. Almost on principle, you might say.

'That's a hefty fine at the very least,' said Charmian tartly. 'You're all mad.'

As she got into her car, she remembered one last question: 'Kate, is your father smoking much these days?'

'Well, he gave it up. But I think he's gone back. Just the odd cigar.'

The Incident Room was in the church hall behind the row of shops in Merrywick, not far from the undertakers and even nearer the mortuary. The street in which it lay was not particularly near the Thames although it was called River Walk, but the developer of Merrywick had had a taste for romantic names that advertised well. The building was new and warmly heated which endeared it to Inspector Elman who felt the cold even more than the damp. The Incident Room was set up with the skill that Fred Elman usually deployed. He prided himself on it. A well organised MIRIAM is the mark of a good investigation, he said. Fall down on that and you've lost yourself at the very beginning of a case. He was right, of course. And lucky to have a Force behind him that was provided with all the computers, word processors, fax machines and telephones that he needed. A lot of funds had been spent on that sort of equipment lately and Elman used them to the full. He was a man who liked his work.

At the moment, though, his feelings were mixed. Murder was murder, a major enquiry demanding all his skills, but he couldn't help wishing that he had been investigating the theft of the Duchess's jewels instead. Now that was a case with promotion prospects if you scored. (And he would have taken pains to see that he did score. Some villain would have gone down for that, if he killed himself.)

But Arthur Franklin was coming down from the Met, he was a specialist. Must remember to find out if the Daniels woman knew him, she seemed to know everyone, and could tell them about his little ways. It paid to find out. Elman liked Daniels, in his careful way, but it was as well to know about the other side of Daniels too. She'd killed a man once, you always had to remember that about her. In the way of duty, naturally, but still, she had done it.

On her way to River Walk, Charmian drove past the Keyright Employment Agency and remembered that she would be asking about Nella there. If the case wasn't closed, and maybe even if it was. There was something about Nella that nagged at her so that she wanted to know more. The girl deserved an obituary.

The moment she walked into the Incident Room, she was noticed, and she was aware of it. Not everyone looked at her, but a current ran through the room. They were all there, she observed: Chief Inspector Father, Inspector Elman and Sergeant Bister. They were grouped around a table in the far corner of the room.

Chief Inspector Father came forward. She had never got on Christian-name terms with him before, but he seemed about to start it. 'Charmian, nice to see you. We're just having some coffee.' He had a sheaf of papers in his hand which he looked down at and then gave a grimace. 'I gather you are totally in the picture about our little problem? Yes, Barstow said she'd spoken to you. Silly girl,' he shook his head. 'But she'll survive. We'll have to see about the other one.'

'Foggerty?'

'Our Marg,' he said heavily. 'Who'd have believed it? Well, we will have to speak to her.'

'But you haven't yet?'

'It's coming.' He was clearly embarrassed and reluctant to talk to her, local dirt should be washed locally, but Daniels was an important lady and almost certainly coming to work in this Force. He had had no confirmation of the appointment but his sources were good and it looked almost certain to him that he was speaking to the new head of a new unit to beat crime. A new powerbase, in short. A pity, in his opinion, to give it to a woman, it ought to be a man, but that was the way society was going.

So he smiled. 'We're checking things out, Jake Henley among them. He was picked up in Cheasey this morning.'

'Good.'

'I gather you've had a bit of trouble yourself?'

Charmian shrugged. 'I'm not sure if there is a connection with all this, but there could be.'

'We'll be looking into it, I promise you. And you'll have extra protection in Maid of Honour Row.'

A duty patrol car at regular intervals taking a look? 'I'm not sure if I want that.'

'Better be safe . . . By the way, Bister's got something to tell you.'

Sergeant Bister cleared his throat. 'You'll be glad to know, ma'am, that the gun I took off Miss Cooper is certainly not the gun that killed Nella Fisher. She's in the clear there.'

'I'm glad.'

'Thought you would be,' and he smiled, revealing excellent white teeth and a pleasant expression. 'Mind you, she should have had a licence.'

And there was Jack, out in the countryside with more than one unlicensed gun, thought Charmian.

Father broke in. 'We'll give her a slap over the wrist for that, but probably not take it any further.'

'She got it off her father,' said Charmian bluntly. 'He has other guns.'

'A gun collector, eh? One of those. Unlicensed every one, I bet. Well, we'll take it up.' He looked at Elman. 'Your job, Fred.'

Elman nodded. 'Wellington Yard, isn't it?'

'You won't find him at home. He does take off sometimes. He has now.'

'Lucky fellow,' said Father. 'Never managed it myself. Fred will land him. Any idea where to look?'

'I don't think he's far away. Try the bars in Windsor and Slough. Or Cheasey. He might be there.'

They talked for a short while, going over the details of the case with all the complications of threats and double-dealing. Nella Fisher, Jake Henley, Dolly Barstow and Kate Cooper together with Jack and Annie, these were the characters in the story, but Margery Foggerty now had the leading part.

Margery Foggerty had been centre-stage ever since declaring herself to be on the spot, near to Nella, almost at the time of the killing, and in a manner that certainly did look like a confession. Lots of criminals, in the end, wanted to be heard, Foggerty might be one such. On the whole, little as he liked the idea, Father wanted the case cleared up quickly. He did not want another suspect.

After Charmian left, with expressions of goodwill and co-operation all round, Chief Inspector Father said:

'We'll have to call in Foggerty.'

'She's had a day off,' said Elman. 'I checked. Personal leave. I think she just wants to get her hair dyed.' It had been showing a bit at the roots.

'Get her in tomorrow. See what she's got to say.' Father shook his head. 'I still can't believe it of Marg.' They had all known her a long time, known her former husband, thought him a brute but liked her. Sad.

In the late afternoon of that October day, Charmian drove towards what was, for her, the most important appointment of the day. Important to her anyway. Might be a matter of life and death.

'Although I certainly trust not,' she told herself as she parked her car near Wimpole Street. She took it as a good sign that she had found a slot and a parking meter.

She had chosen a physician who had his practice in London, not too far from her office. Experience had taught that it was better to have a doctor who did not live in the same neighbourhood. In her profession it was wiser. This particular doctor had been thoroughly vetted by Security and could be trusted.

He had one other virtue: he never kept his patients waiting. Appointments were honoured on time. He had no bedside manner or charm as such, but he listened. She valued that.

Now he took in what she had to say about her symptoms,

before answering in a gentle, quiet voice. Behind his professional voice he had the remains of a South London accent, and she liked this, too. Someone who made his own life.

'Just a quick examination,' he murmured.

He had an agreeable examination room with a middle-aged nurse whom Charmian liked. They had met several times when she had been recovering from an attempted murder and rape. She had killed her attacker, and had taken longer to get over the backlash than she liked to admit.

When the examination was completed, and not much in it and nothing to fear, her doctor suggested an appointment with a specialist.

'I think it's nothing more than an aberration of the ovaries. But perhaps we should check. Peskett's a good man. So is Dunkeld. We trained together at Tommy's.'

Charmian thought about it. Then she heard herself say: 'I think I'd prefer a woman.'

No successful, intellectual career lady should say such a thing. You should go for the best in the field, sex did not matter.

But suddenly, for her, it did.

Threats on all sides, she thought.

Jake Henley, the vitriol, Jack and his guns. Perhaps a woman was safer with women.

Except that Nella Fisher might not have been safer with Sergeant Margery Foggerty.

# CHAPTER NINE

## *Wednesday, October 11*

Margery Foggerty returned to her flat in Merrywick Parade after her visit to the hairdresser's with her hair neatly coiffed and tinted her usual pale beige but not happy.

Her father had been in the Guards so she knew the tradition that you died with your boots clean. She had been right to have her hair done, but she had the miserable feeling she was about to face professional suicide. Or worse.

Might easily be worse. Well, you took what you wanted and you paid for it. She had taken holidays in Spain, had a nice little bank balance, even a few investments, in return for passing over information that alerted Jake Henley – which was what he called himself lately, although she knew of other names – to police activity that was coming his way.

She thought she would have gone unsuspected for ever if she hadn't been seen by that bloody girl, Nella. Something of a blackmailer, that girl, and they often had short lives. Of course, there was always Barstow, but she thought she could have dealt with Barstow. Loyalties still counted for something.

One of her troubles was that she had liked Jake. Had even fallen in love with him a bit, which had obscured her vision, usually so refined and sharp, of what was right for Sergeant Margery Foggerty. Not seriously in love, of course, just as far as she could fall in love, which was not a lot, but enough to make her a bit silly.

Drinking with him in The Grey Man had been silly. Only the once, but that once, as the girl said to the soldier, was enough.

She was an old and wily enough police officer to have picked up the first faint signals of caution towards her on the part of her senior officers. She was ceasing to be old Marg whom they had known for years and treated as part of the furniture, and becoming Sergeant Foggerty, doubtful character, keep your distance from her because dirt sticks.

She was a kind of disease now, the Foggerty virus, she was catching. No one was nastier than one's peers and equals when it came down to it. Only to be expected.

And I'm not the only rotten apple in their barrel, she told herself with grim amusement. There was the one they called Red Rick.

Now there was this message that Chief Inspector Father wanted to see her. Tomorrow, please, in his room in the Datchet Road station, 11 a.m. sharp.

Probably she wouldn't go. She had cash that no one knew about. She had taken the precaution of opening a bank account in Jersey. Her passport was in order.

She would pack a bag, take a train to London and melt into the big smoke. Only she wouldn't, she would take the Piccadilly Line to Heathrow and fly out to drain her bank account.

After the hairdresser's she had popped into Eddie Dick's employment agency in Merrywick to use his fax machine to get in touch with the bank in St Helier. Eddie had been welcoming as usual. He had nice manners which you had to take with a grain of salt because they might not mean much. His office was busy as ever, even a queue of young women and lads waiting to be interviewed, all nicely dressed; he had attracted the best people in Merrywick. He came round to the alcove where she was using the fax machine to greet her.

'Little bit of business done, Marg?' He had watched her keenly, of course.

It was always a 'little bit of business' with him if you were a woman. His way of implying that a woman couldn't be important. He would probably have said it to Mrs Thatcher. 'Had a nice little day in the House of Commons today, Prime Minister? You've been doing some nice little things with the trade unions.' She would have laughed at him inside, just as Foggerty did, but politely and with a straight face, not letting him know.

She had returned to her house in central Merrywick – a bit hard to abandon it since it was a nice piece of property, but it carried a big mortgage and she hadn't paid off all that much of the purchase price. She could leave it behind. So she started to gather together those possessions she wished to take with her.

Then she made a pot of tea and smoked a cigarette before getting on with the task.

She finished her packing, taking only what she liked most. With any luck she would have time and money to buy a bit of stuff once across the Channel. No one knew, but she had a small flat in Spain. She would head for there, and under another name. Possibly no one would come looking for her. It depended what evidence they had. Jake Henley would not talk.

Pity about tomorrow because she had a date.

She had a kind of boyfriend. Platonic, naturally, she was off the sex stuff. Although they played a kind of game that was sexual in origins. Had to be.

She was never completely sure if he liked 'dating' (he preferred that Americanism, not sure if she did herself) a policewoman. But it might be that she was about the best he could do. After all, not every woman, probably not many at all, would play the game the way she did. Having initiated her into it, he would not want to start all over again with someone else.

As a matter of fact, she enjoyed the game. She'd always liked a uniform. Just a bit of artifice, after all, and she had enjoyed amateur dramatics in her day. No starring part ever, just a walk-on or a few lines. But now she had a leading role.

Well, there had to be a reason why she had been attracted to him. But after all, you never really knew why you fell into things.

The game they played didn't go on all night. After they'd had dinner (they always had dinner, probably the only time he ate much), they reverted to being themselves and talking normally. Always plenty to talk about.

She had really enjoyed their little evenings. But she'd had the last.

Time hanging on her hands as it always did just before a journey, she decided to start a letter. To put her point of view, how it had been for her. Women didn't always get much of a chance to do this, and if she went to prison, and it might come to that although she hoped not, she certainly wouldn't get much chance there.

She knew Tony Father better than some, had known him for a long time. She would write to him.

Dear Tony, she began.

When the doorbell rang she was surprised, considered not answering the door, but in the end she opened it.

He was there. In costume.

'Oh Colonel Vanderpest,' she said coyly. This was her joke name for him. 'I wasn't expecting you. Not dressed like that. I didn't know you.' Which was a silly thing to say, because she obviously had. 'And why are you wearing that great shiny rain cape? Officers don't wear those.'

'It's raining,' said the Colonel gruffly. 'Mustn't get the uniform wet. Shan't get another. Or not easily.' From underneath the big cape came a muffled bark.

'Got Trixie with you, have you?' It was said without pleasure, Marg was not a dog-lover. 'She must be stifled under there. Come in now, but you mustn't stay long. Things to do.' She waved her hands in the air. 'My God, that cigar's a bit rank. It'll kill you yet. I didn't think Eisenhower smoked cigars.' She usually flattered him. He liked to be thought of as a four-star general and he often took on the role of Eisenhower, or General Marshall or that chap who got sacked by the President. 'Or you going to be Patton tonight? He was a real killer now.'

Killer diller, she said to herself. Killer diller.

# CHAPTER TEN

## *The early hours of Thursday, October 12*

After her appointment in Wimpole Street, Charmian went to her office where she worked late into the evening. Then she walked round the corner to her favourite Italian restaurant to eat a solitary supper. She liked Italian food and Italian wine, both were generous and warm like their country of origin. She only ate Chinese or Indian food under protest.

I'm a European at heart, she told herself as she sipped some Orvieto, and waited for the minestrone to appear. You had to wait for your food at Aldo's, that it was its only drawback. The proprietor, Maria, a middle-aged woman from a London-Italian family of long standing, claimed it was because all the food was freshly cooked, and sometimes this was probably true, although not always. Charmian knew for a fact that Maria bought in her puddings and rich cakes, because she had seen the van delivering them. Continental Gourmet Foods, Staines, Middx, it had said.

Maria, a stout but short lady with curly black hair, put down the soup. 'Black pepper? Parmesan?'

Why do the Italians think that the British want gratings of black pepper on everything, Charmian thought. But they do, so perhaps we eat more of it than the rest of Europe. She said no to the pepper and yes to the Parmesan cheese.

'You look pale tonight,' said Maria. She knew exactly who Charmian was and precisely what her rank and status in the police was. Maria operated an excellent intelligence network through her numerous relations, all of whom had lived in this part of London for generations but who went home to the same village in northern Italy for a holiday every summer. They had

British passports and cockney accents but the blood link ran strong. Every time the family party went home they brought a youngster back with them and repatriated an old one with his pension rights to enjoy his retirement in a better climate. Occasionally, a pensioner who preferred English television or had married an English wife refused to go. Maria would be one who would not go, she had a husband who worked for British Airways, she had a daughter doing well in the City, and a son who was a schoolteacher. She was too dug in to leave, although never feeling English.

'Just tired,' said Charmian.

'You work too hard. It is bad for women.'

Bad for our looks, thought Charmian, catching a glimpse of herself in the wall mirror, not a trace of lipstick and hair a mess. 'Bad for everyone,' she said.

'My daughter also works too hard. You will never a get a husband, I say to her, but I think she does not want one. She has a big flat, a smart car and lots of expensive clothes, she says a husband would be a luxury she cannot afford.'

Charmian drove home, deliberately taking a route that took her through Cheasey. There was quite a lot of night-life in Cheasey, as she remembered from past years. She noted a police car and an ambulance with a flashing blue light outside the Youth Centre in Addison Street; such a scene was about average for the place and time of night. Always trouble at the Youth Centre. The big disco club in Oxford Road was going strong with flashing lights inside and out but was otherwise peaceful. They had several good bouncers who kept things under control.

She drove past The Grey Man. Lights out there, and all dark. But slipped into the carpark at the side was a long, flashy-looking car that she would take a bet belonged to Jake Henley. Might be worth checking. Rewley could do that for her later if she got the number. She slowed down but found she still could not read the registration number.

She stopped the car at the kerb and walked across to see. It was dark in the carpark, a deeper pocket of shadow where the car stood. She bent forward to look.

As she did so, the car door opened and Jake Henley got

out. 'Ah, the lady detective.' He advanced a pace. 'Looking for something?'

Charmian stood her ground. 'Cars parked in the dark beside The Grey Man are always worth looking at. Why were you sitting in the car?'

'Thinking, darling. I do think, you know.'

Someone somewhere had told her that Jake was an educated man, had had a year at university before going into crime. Or going back into it; the records suggested that he had been a practised criminal from about the age of eight. Prone to fits of sudden violence too.

'You must have plenty to think about.'

'If you mean the offer, none too delicately put to me by Elman, that if I confessed to killing Nella Fisher, he would see what he could do for me, I didn't have to think about that. No, ma'am.' His tone was savage. 'You're not going to fit me up with that one.'

She doubted if the worldly and cautious Elman had made any such blunt offer, but something had obviously been said. Charmian did not move. To have taken a step back would have looked like retreat, to have taken one forward would have been interpreted as aggression.

They were close enough for her to smell the drink on his breath. Stalemate, she thought. Stupidly she had got herself into a position which she would have warned the youngest recruit to the force to avoid. Never go into anything, she would have said, without knowing the way out. Strength for strength, she was no match for Jake Henley if he wanted to try anything. When it came down to it, men were stronger than most women.

He stretched out his hands, not touching her, but extending his fingers stiffly like rods as if he wanted to ram them into her body. Her friends, Winfred Eagle and Birdie Peacock, had taught her that this gesture warded off a foe. But Charmian doubted if Jake was into witchcraft. With him it was a straight gesture of animal hostility. He hated her.

They stood there for a moment, looking at each other. Eye contact was dangerous with a man about to attack, she knew that, but she was held.

105

Then the police car from the Youth Centre passed down the road, light still flashing. The moment was broken. He gave her an exit himself.

'If you will just shift your car, I can back out,' he said. 'You're blocking me.'

Silently, Charmian turned to her car. I lost that one, she thought, and was furious. I would like to have hit him, she acknowledged. If he had touched me I would have had an excuse to hit him hard.

She watched Henley back his car out, swing it round and drive off in the opposite direction, much too fast.

Charmian drove more sedately towards Merrywick and thence home.

A mile of open farmland with cattle-grids, followed by the parkland of a mansion now the property of a soap company, stretched between Cheasey and Merrywick. The moon was up and the night clear. She drove fast through a landscape of magical beauty, silvered and quiet.

Then the road curved and she was in Merrywick.

People went to bed early in Merrywick but there were lights on in some windows. It was interesting, she thought, that however late you were out, there was always someone still awake. A few insomniacs in Merrywick. Kate and Dolly not amongst them, she noted, all lights out in 33A and 33B Didcot Square. It was possible, of course, that Kate was in Wellington Yard with her mother. And where was Jack?

As she drove past the small parade of shops which curved in a half-moon opposite the church, she saw a man walking his dog on the grass border.

But he wasn't walking. He was standing between two flower-beds and was staring down at the dog. He seemed to be looking around him in bewilderment, rubbing his hands up and down his jacket as if to clean them.

As she got closer she saw who it was: Edward Dick, the owner and manager of the Keyright Employment Agency. She did not know him well, but they had met once or twice.

She stopped the car. 'What's wrong?' He looked at her but did not answer. She saw that he was shivering, but not with cold. It was a warm if damp night.

106

'Don't get out of the car,' he said, his voice thick. The dog lifted its head and howled, one long sad note.

She ignored this order. 'What's wrong with the dog?' Without waiting for an answer she knelt down by the animal to see for herself. The dog, it was a dog, not a bitch, a little spaniel, was breathing heavily.

She lifted up one paw which was stained with blood. 'He's cut himself. There's blood on his paw.'

Edward Dick grabbed the dog and clutched it to him, it was still making whimpering noises. 'No, not cut. Stood in it. Stood in blood. I was just bringing him out for his little walk. I'm out twice a night, you know.' He looked down at his feet. 'I've stood in blood. Now you've knelt in blood.' He was just managing to keep his voice steady. 'There shouldn't be any blood there, you know. I don't know how it got there.'

Charmian stood up. He was quite right. A circle of blood now stained her long pleated skirt where she had knelt on the earth. There must be large patch of blood on the grass, although it was difficult to see in the shadows from the moon and the streetlights. She put her hand on the grass; it felt wet, but that might be from the rain earlier in the evening. When she looked at her hand, she saw there was blood on her fingers.

The dog had walked in it, she had knelt in it, and Eddie Dick had wiped it down his coat, and now she had it on her hand. They were all stained.

'It might be from an injured animal.' She looked around the grass on the roadway, but there was no sign of one. The little spaniel seemed unharmed. But another injured animal could have crawled away to die. On the other hand, it could be human blood.

'Go back home, Mr Dick,' she ordered. He looked sick, but the blood was not from him, nor from the spaniel, who seemed to rejoice in the name of Henry. 'And I will look around.'

'No.'

'Do what I say, please. Just leave it all to me.' She knew he lived over the shop and they were standing just in front of the Keyright office. He must have been on the point of going home when he and Henry walked into the blood.

When he had reluctantly obeyed her, she marked out what

seemed to be the area of bloody grass with stones gathered from the flowerbeds. Then she picked up her car phone and called the main station on the Didcot Road. The blood might be anything, it might be nothing, but she wanted to know.

She sat on the grass verge until the patrol car arrived, then she pointed out the blood and explained what had happened. One of the uniformed policeman studied the grass. 'Looks as though someone or something has stood here or been placed here and bled. The grass is dented a bit. Doesn't look heavy enough or big enough for a body.' He added: 'Not a big body or a whole body.'

'Shut up, Jim,' said his companion.

'Just thinking.'

'It might be something. Hard to say, ma'am,' said DC Jimpson. He knew Charmian of course. 'But I'll mark out the area and cover it with a bit of plastic and report what I've done.'

'There's more blood over here. Traces, anyway,' called the other man, DC Thomas, who had moved further afield. 'And here.'

'Right, I'll mark those too.'

It was beginning to look more serious.

'Can't do much more, ma'am, until morning,' he said.

'Leave you to it,' said Charmian, as she drove off, leaving behind her what appeared to be one of those little mysteries that might be solved or might not, leading either to something or to nothing.

She was reasonably content with the way things were going. The picture was that Margery Foggerty had killed Nella Fisher, probably in a panic. A stupid crime. Charmian had only met Foggerty briefly, but she had seemed a stupid woman. Jake Henley was on the loose, and not a nice man, but that was a problem that could be dealt with. If he was a threat to her, then she knew how to look after herself. Jack Cooper, she thought, was a nuisance, no more, he would turn up again. Kate was in the clear, thank goodness, she loved Kate.

Early morning reveries, whether happy or troubled, are not usually good indicators of the true position. Charmian knew this fact as well as anyone, but private worries apart, she was optimistic.

As she drove through the back streets of Windsor to Maid of Honour Row, she passed, unknowing, the room in which Jack Cooper lay abed. He had got himself a room in the house of a drinking companion who was glad to help out a pal, and might ask the same favour himself one day if the wife ever came back. She had left in a huff three weeks ago but might return any minute now. Meanwhile Jack was in the spare room where he lay looking at the ceiling and not sleeping. In this after-midnight hour, insomniac and with a bad headache, he was thinking how he hated Charmian Daniels and what a nuisance she was in his life. His legs twitched as if they wanted to go for a walk. Should he get up and go bang on her door? Bang on her head. Bang . . . He lay there fantasising. His friends' dog, a nice little mongrel bitch, who had taken a fancy to Jack who was better at taking her for walks than her master, lay across his legs and moaned, whether in pleasure or pain Jack could not decide.

Charmian drove on, parked her car and let herself into her warm, safe house, unaware of how close she had come to destruction that night.

When morning dawned, the trail of blood was seen to stretch across the grass and then to stop. In daylight it looked as though something or someone had been dragged across from the direction of a row of houses and flats to the west of the shopping area.

The police decided to do a house-to-house enquiry.

# CHAPTER ELEVEN

## *Daylight on Thursday, October 12*

The young detective constable, his breakfast still in his mouth, who was pacing the grass as he checked for blood traces, discovered that the splatters of red carried on towards the pavement in front of the row of houses and flats – called Merrywick Parade – that lay just beyond the row of shops. It was all grass here, with a few shrubs and old trees because only ten years ago this had been open country, part of a farm. He half remembered it from boyhood. Cows, he thought, and once a circus camped out here, with lions in cages, and rotting meat they left behind to stink the air. He remembered the smell vividly.

On the pavement he thought he saw the traces of a bloody footprint. Beyond that, nothing.

'Someone walked in blood here. Then whoever it was went on the grass, either dripping blood or carrying something that dripped blood.'

Perhaps a butcher going home. Sick joke, no, he didn't mean that, wipe it out. Someone carrying an injured animal? Or a chap who had been out shooting and had pheasants or rabbits slung from his bag. That would drip blood. There was a bit of shooting in the woods and fields around.

Not at night, said a sceptical voice inside him.

He marked out the largest area of blood, which he covered with a piece of plastic. After this, he drew a map on which he indicated all the spots where blood had been found. Then he took careful samples from several sites and sealed the envelopes. If it wasn't human blood that would be the end of it. And possibly even if it was – unless a body or a victim turned up.

He was anxious to do a good job, having only just transferred from the uniformed branch.

There didn't seem to be any more blood around. That was the end of it. He had done all he could.

Jimpson looked at his colleague who was pacing along the road towards him. 'Found anything?'

'Nothing here.'

The two young men consulted. The one who had been to the other end of the road and found nothing, said: 'What do we do now? Do we just stand here guarding that patch of blood you have so carefully marked out? Look proper Charlies, won't we?'

'We'll report back and see what the boss says.'

'Waste of time. Let's just go back.'

'Let's both take one more look up the road,' said the first young man. He was the determined one of the two.

'We'll attract attention.'

'It's the job. Come on, Tommy.'

It was true. Already a few early risers had noticed them but had walked on, not without interest, but not lingering. Trains had to be caught. A man standing in his front garden openly staring at them, while a boy delivering the morning papers stood beside the postman watching them with wide eyes.

'You do it, I'm going back to the car.' DC Thomas returned to his seat at the wheel and stared straight ahead of him. If Jumbo wanted to be like that, let him.

After a while, he turned to see what Jumbo was up to. Jimpson was standing with his hand on the gate of a house. Then he slowly walked up the garden path and rang the doorbell.

DC Thomas watched. No one answered the door. 'Gone to work, you silly sod,' he said, settling back into his seat. 'Or in bed. Wish I was.' DC Jimpson was bending down and looking through the letterbox. Then he swung round and marched back to the car.

He got in and sat down beside Thomas. 'Get through to the boss,' he said.

'Why?'

Jimpson held out his hand. His right palm had a dark-brown smear on it. 'There was blood on that gate. I tried the house but no one answered. So I looked through the letterbox.' He

111

took a deep breath. 'It smells. The house smells bad. Like dead meat.' Memories of his boyhood came flooding back to turn his stomach. He steadied down. 'Radio back. Get hold of Bister. Find out who lives there. We've got to get in.'

DC Thomas took him seriously. He spoke across radio: 'Sarge?'

Charmian, still ignorant of how close to a death she had been, prepared a large breakfast (how strange to want to be getting fatter when a large part of her life had been devoted to staying slim) and fed her cat Muff who had never had any inhibitions one way or another and believed that food was there for the eating.

She ringed round the date of her appointment with the specialist on the wall calendar (the October picture of a huge, grinning ginger cat was cheering): only a week to wait. How speedy they had been. A bad sign?

Last night, she had avoided her telephone and any messages the answering machine might have waiting for her, but now she ran them through.

George Rewley spoke first, using his official voice: 'We expect to be questioning a suspect in the Fisher killing tomorrow.' Prudently, he did not name the suspect but Charmian knew he meant Sergeant Foggerty. 'The prospect of clearing up the case looks good.' There was a pause, then he said: 'Thought you would like to know that I've seen Kate, she seems in a better mood, and she is moving back into her own place. I'm going round there to see her.'

Kate got in next: 'Just to tell you I will be back in the flat tomorrow. Dad's been sighted in a bar in Peascod Street. No word from him to us, of course, but things are looking brighter. Dolly has hinted that they might have found somebody for Nella's death. Hope so. I'll ring tomorrow.'

Finally, Dolly Barstow spoke. 'Kate and I have had an almighty row. Sharp things said on either side, but as a result the air is now cleared and we both feel better. She really likes George Rewley and I can't blame her for that. She will be back in Didcot Square tomorrow and we are going to have a drink on it. Talking of drink, I know, but Kate may not, that Jack is lodging with an old mate in East Windsor, and is drinking heavily. Seen walking someone's dog. Not his own. Said to be in a bad mood, and making threats. Probably just drink, but better stay away from him.'

Well, thanks, thought Charmian, tell me how. But she dismissed apprehension as she got herself ready for the day. Women react to what they wear. Men do as well, which is why they wear uniform of one sort to another so often; it makes them feel good to match other men. Now Charmian dressed for alertness and positive action. A black leather skirt made in Italy (she had good legs and could afford to show them), and a long cashmere sweater in bright red. She would be occupying her London office where it would be a hard-working day with committees, two meetings with colleagues, and a visit from an MP who wanted information. With him, she would have to be guarded, his motives were suspect. He was a man on the make.

Muff followed her to watch the dressing process. A small operation in her youth had rendered her sexless, but Muff remained resolutely female. Actively interested indeed, since a tiny piece of ovarian tissue, of the type now possibly proving so worrying to her owner, had been left inside and several times a year caused her to be courted by a large circle of Windsor cats. It was thought she favoured several males, choosing not by looks but by some private, arbitrary taste of her own.

Now she sat on the bed studying her mistress, although that was the wrong word, because she controlled Charmian rather than the other way round. On the bed was Charmian's nightgown. She was ashamed of it really, no one ought to wear a nightgown so old that it was falling apart. It was good silk, she had bought it in Paris. Paid for it herself, no man had given it to her, and she had worn it happily for years. But the lace was threading apart and the seams disintegrating.

Muff moved herself on to the silk and kneaded it with her paws, she put her nose down on it, purring. Her enthusiasm carried her away so that her claws caught on the lace and she got more and more entangled. As she struggled to get free, the silk began to wind itself around her throat. She was still purring, she was still enjoying herself, but she was shredding the silk. Her look grew serious as she got tied up in the silk and her back legs became hobbled. Then she caught Charmian's eyes and screamed for help. Fury had replaced happiness in a flash.

Charmian shook her head ruefully: 'You and I are more like each other than we are both like men.'

She disentangled the cat, now stretching out angry unhelpful claws, and shut the door on her. But she was amused. The ridiculousness of it all was part of life.

I shall have to be careful, she told herself, or I shall start laughing again. She hadn't laughed properly for a long while now.

She tidied the house, said a soothing word to the cat, and sped off to London.

Behind her in Windsor, events were moving in a way no one could have predicted. The telephone started to ring in her house in Maid of Honour Row. First Dolly Barstow, then Sergeant George Rewley, then Bister came on the line, and finally Inspector Fred Elman himself.

But Charmian's early work schedule took her to appointments outside her own office. She was not to be found.

Inspector Fred Elman was a man who usually thought about himself first. He did it quite unconsciously, so naturally that even his wife did not notice what he was doing. What suited him just came first.

Now, as he looked down on the dead body on the floor in the house in Merrywick Parade, he thought that he had been spared a long wait to interview someone who was not going to turn up. It was today they had been due to talk. Wouldn't have been an easy interview.

'Yes, it's Marg,' he said, turning away, more moved than he liked to show. 'Who'd have thought she'd get herself killed?'

He stood in silence for a moment, studying the scene.

'No chance of it being suicide?'

Sergeant Bister shook his head. 'No powder marks and no gun.'

Margery Foggerty lay on the ground in the hall, her face half turned towards the front door. The central heating had been on full power and her body had rested against a radiator, the heat of which had brought out the smell of death. It was sweet and strong in the hall.

114

She had been shot once in the head and once in the chest. Either wound would have killed her. She had bled profusely and blood was everywhere.

'Must have spouted out,' said Elman. 'Poor cow. What a business.'

Bister, who had been on the scene early and spoken to the police surgeon who had delivered the unnecessary judgement that she was dead, said: 'Hit an artery while the heart was still beating. The killer probably got blood on him. Or whatever he was wearing. That'll be a help.'

'Unless he was naked.'

'Not this one,' said Bister with conviction. Every so often that notion came up, started with Lizzie Borden, he thought, but he had never known a case proved.

There were two suitcases in the hall.

'She was packing to go away,' said Bister.

'I reckon,' said Elman. 'Running away. Did she kill the Fisher girl? Had she got a gun? Have you had a look?'

'Looking now,' said Bister briefly. 'We're turning everything over.'

'Wonder what type of gun killed her?'

The two men looked at each other, they were both thinking the same thing.

'We won't know,' said Elman, 'until Doc Palmer does the PM and digs the bullets out.' He was regretful. He liked Dr Palmer but no one could say he hurried himself. When questioned he claimed he was overworked.

Bister, accomplished at reading Fred Elman, saw all this. 'One bullet went wide and hit the wall.' He indicated a damaged patch. 'I've sent it off to Ballistics. Jim Gold is doing it.'

'Good. A good chap, Jim, and a quick worker.'

'I suggested Jim might like to compare it with the bullet that killed Nella Fisher,' said Bister carefully.

There was a pause.

'Good,' said Elman. 'You're right. I've never liked coincidences.'

Elman was so cheered by this thought that he took Bister and George Rewley, who arrived at that moment, to the Royal Arms on the village green at Merrywick for a drink and a talk.

'I could do with a drink. Come on, both of you.' He liked both Bister and Rewley.

Elman was more at his ease with men than with women, and George Rewley, who was better than most at reading the messages written in invisible ink, understood that between Margery Foggerty and Fred Elman there must have been a passage. Marg Foggerty was known to have the reputation of being one with the lads. Put herself about, as the saying goes.

Elman had taken his place in the line-up and was probably somewhat ashamed of the memory. Alarmed, too. Women were powerful and threatening deities who could only be subdued by sexual force. A bad case of male unease. There was a lot of that in the Force.

So he spoke of not liking coincidences. It was better than saying he didn't know how to handle his feelings but wanted to do his best for Marg.

'Poor old Marg,' he said over his beer, thus reducing her powers one degree more by his pity. 'She wasn't a bad sort. Got into bad ways, that's all.' He took a deep draught. 'I hope we get her killer.'

Then his last mouthful of beer seemed to turn sour.

'Amazing, isn't it, that Daniels should be the one to find the blood? She gets everywhere.'

Sergeant Rewley preserved a tactful silence. Bister grinned.

Elman stood up. 'Drink up, I'll get us some more.' When he returned, he sat down heavily. It was a positive movement, indicating to Rewley that something was to come. It was not just a sitting down, it was a statement: Listen to me.

'I expect you've heard the rumours about Daniels? You hear everything. She's about to honour us with her presence.' Elman did not approve of women in authority and Charmian had too much of that already. 'There's going to be a reshuffle, a rearrangement. A regrouping, they call it. What it is, is a chance to get rid of those whose faces don't fit. A completely new unit called SCRADIC is going to be created.'

Bister wondered where Elman got his gossip from but guessed it was correct. He'd heard a bit himself. Rewley did not wonder because he knew: Elman's wife worked in the secretariat.

'And Daniels is going to be offered the number two spot. They like her face, you see.'

'So we'll have to be good boys and let her in on this?' said Bister.

Couldn't keep her out, thought Elman. His spies had told him that Charmian might not accept the job. Swithering, was the phrase used, she being a Scots girl. Or was she bargaining for the top spot of all? That also was being speculated.

The beer suddenly tasted flat and sour to Bister. Somehow he saw his chances of promotion altering radically. He had worked out the odds and now the odds had been changed.

'I'd like it to be Jake Henley for this,' said Elman in a brooding voice. 'But I don't suppose we'll get him for it. He always slides away from things. Only once has he been inside and that was for a porn deal and even then he didn't get what he should have done. Poxy judge giving him the benefit of the doubt.'

Their drinking did not last long. Elman went back to the Incident Room in the church hall to see what new information, if any, had come in on the Nella Fisher case, and Bister went off to see what Ballistics were up to, while George Rewley took himself back to the house in Merrywick Parade.

He was glad to see that the crowd of onlookers had diminished because of the rain, now falling steadily. Methodical samples were being taken of the grass where it was stained, and the larger area of bloody turf was marked out and carefully covered. Forensics were going to remove the whole top layer for examination in the laboratory. But blood being blood – and you could never tell who was HIV positive these days – they were being very very careful. In his experience, all scientists were very careful of themselves and Rewley for one did not blame them.

As he entered the house, from which the body of Sergeant Margery Foggerty was just being removed, the telephone rang.

The message was for him, and it was from Bister who had spoken to the Ballistics expert. The other bullet that had been found in the murder room had blood on it too, but probably too little to offer much to Forensics. So possibly the killer had been hit too, probably from the shot that ricocheted.

But the crucial news was in his next sentence. The bullet had certain characteristics that identified the type of gun used. The gun which had killed Margery Foggerty was the same as that which had killed Nella Fisher.

A revolver, of a type handed out to American servicemen during the war. A GI gun.

Moving rapidly around her London circuit, it took some time for messages to catch up with Charmian. Interestingly, it was Dolly Barstow who got the news to Charmian first.

Charmian was in the middle of one of her rare luxury lunches. Usually she ate nothing, or fish and chips in a police canteen somewhere. It all depended. But that day, she was eating with a journalist who wanted to interview with her. So the journalist, who had simple ideas and thought you could bribe people with food, had taken her to Langan's.

They were sitting waiting for a spinach soufflé to get itself blown up into a puff with hot air, when the telephone was put on their table.

With the journalist listening avidly and making mental notes, Charmian took the call.

'Listen, Foggerty's been shot dead. And by the same gun that killed Nella Fisher.'

It was the only news that could have taken her mind off her food. The case was wide open.

Margery Foggerty had been dead for nearly twenty-four hours by the time Charmian Daniels walked in on the scene. Her body had been removed but the smell hung about and a bluebottle had appeared.

Charmian flapped it away angrily. George Rewley watched her. Elman had left him in charge, Bister now being otherwise occupied – those jewels were keeping everyone busy – with the added brief to keep an eye on Daniels. Which he would have done anyway since he was now seriously in love with Kate, who was her godchild. Kate was back in her own flat and washing her hair. That was a good sign. A girl with clean hair is a good girl who will not run away.

The bluebottle buzzed in her face. 'Get some fly spray,' said Charmian fiercely. 'It's disgusting.' Her skin was crawling.

'Is there any other connection between this murder and Nella's, except the gun?'

'There is one other thing.' Rewley led the way into the kitchen. 'We didn't see it straight away. I don't know why. Too obvious, maybe.'

On the table, scrawled in blood, was the word WOMEN. It had dried badly but it was readable. The writer had not needed to write BLOODY WOMEN because he had written in blood.

For the moment, that was all and that was enough. Nella and Margery Foggerty were two islands, but the whole world of corruption and pornography spread out like a bridge, joining them up. Cheasey was a kind of archipelago floating on the moving crust of the earth towards them.

Charmian surveyed the house, which had been photographed and searched and over which an exhausted silence now hung. A small army had been in there and had now passed on, leaving their mark behind them.

Now the men were outside, dealing with the bloodstained grass where Charmian had first seen traces. She had started it all there.

Edward Dick had been questioned and offered what he knew, which was not much. His spaniel dog, the questioner reported, carried no wound. Mr Dick had already despatched to the cleaner's the jacket on which he had wiped his hands, for which you couldn't blame him, the questioner added.

The rain had stopped and the plastic sheeting had been removed. Two members of the Forensic unit were carefully peeling away the turf. They would go down a few feet to make sure they had everything, making a clean job of it. Slowly the grass was rolled back, and the dark earth was revealed. Another foot, still further down. The digging had disturbed something. Worms moved, brown and pink, insects hurried for cover.

'Wait,' Charmian knelt down. She could see a gleam of brownish-white. She touched it delicately with a pencil.

A bone.

She touched it again. As the earth fell away, other bones could be seen, clearly human. Fingers pointing upward, a circle of wristbones. A skull with empty eyes full of damp earth from which an insect crawled.

They had found another body.

# CHAPTER TWELVE

## Sunday, October 15

The sober and respectable citizens of Windsor, Eton and Merrywick took the discovery of another body with shock. They felt a sense of outrage. The murder of Nella Fisher had been absorbed with interest and some pity, but after all, she came from Cheasey and everyone knew about Cheasey. However, the death of WS Margery Foggerty was received in respectful silence since it was known that the police lived different lives and might face different pressures. A lot of people (although none of those who had known Marg herself) assumed it must be suicide. But when the bones were uncovered in the earth of what had once been a meadow, there was an unpleasant sensation. Not exactly alarm, but a feeling that this should not be happening here. The inhabitants of Merrywick felt a particular distaste for murder on their doorstep: it might lower the value of property.

Some people, of course, frankly enjoyed it.

Old Mrs Beadle, one of the few truly old inhabitants of Merrywick, since she had lived all her life in her cottage and seen the building of the smart squares and terraces on what had been farmland, found it an entertainment beyond her expectations. A television crew had arrived to film the scene, a radio car was parked, apparently permanently, outside her door, she had fed the crew tea and they had interviewed her. Not that she had much information – although plenty to say – but she reckoned she must have been living in her house when what she called 'the first corpse' had been buried.

The time it took for a dead body to be stripped down to bone varied according to all sorts of factors, such as the nature of the soil, the way it was buried and the activity of animal and bacterial life upon the flesh. The police Forensic team was working on that aspect of the enquiry, as also on the question of the dead person's identity. But the neighbourhood gossips were not waiting on official stories.

Rumour said that the corpse was male, had been dead at least eight to ten years, possibly longer, and had been wearing flared jeans. The fashion-conscious dated the burying by that detail of styling.

No one as yet knew how he had been killed, and even the sex of the victim might be open to doubt because a widely circulated sub-rumour suggested it was a woman. Another rumour hinted that there might yet be other bodies to be found. But rumour did not know everything.

Asked to name some other old inhabitant who could be interviewed, Mrs Beadle offered up Eddie Dick of the Keyright Employment Agency for whose parents she had worked in what she called 'the old days'. She still did his laundry for him, although he dabbed a few bits out himself, although better if he didn't, she added sardonically. But Edward Dick puckered his lips and declined to say much. Not good for business. In any case, even if he had been living there at the time of the burial in what had been, if his memory served, a field full of cows, he had not witnessed it and he hoped he did not know the dead person.

In Cheasey there was plenty of guarded comment about the death of Margery Foggerty, known as she was there and not liked.

'Asking for it, I reckon,' said Ginny, the hostess of The Grey Man.

'Asking for something any rate,' agreed her partner, their exact relationship being a mystery and a cause for speculation among the customers. They slept in separate rooms, both wore wedding rings and in certain lights did look remarkably alike. Twins, someone said. There were occasional jokes about cross-dressing. Did they or didn't they? There were no ready answers.

'Seen Jake lately?'

It was a loaded question. He was keeping a low profile,

not exactly hiding but not putting himself around. He had been briefly taken in and questioned by the police and then released without a charge. No evidence, you couldn't hang a man on talk, not these days as his lawyer had pointed out smartly. Not that anyone got hung. Fifteen years inside at the most.

About the skeleton there was public silence. In private it was possible that names were being bandied about. A certain percentage of the population of Cheasey went missing every year: usually for thoroughly understood motives like debt, threat of police prosecution or desertion of a spouse. Death was not usually suspected but could always be imagined. Cheasey could imagine anything. Almost every family group in Cheasey had one or two absentees but the Fisher-Rivers-Waters-Seaman clan had several. They would be hard put to recognise some of them by now.

There was no reason to believe the skeleton came from that neighbourhood at all.

Why not London? The police opinion was wide open. Three days had passed without any strong body of opinion being formed about the bones. There was no connection, both Inspector Elman and Chief Inspector Father believed, between the skeleton and the murders in Merrywick except place and the timing of the discovery. The two men were meeting in the Incident Room in River Walk, where the investigation into the two murders, now seen as one case, was being conducted. It was Sunday, but it was a working day. They were short of staff and short of resources. As usual.

Consequently the mood in the MIRIAM room was not happy. Why bones as well? was the feeling.

'Another one of those coincidences,' grumbled Elman. 'No other connection. All the same, an odd little item they turned up with the bones. Wonder if he really wore it and why.' He was interested. 'A bit naff,' he said, almost wistfully. 'Ought to help identify him.'

Father refused to be drawn. The skeleton represented just a nuisance he could have done without, a complication in a life already complicated by life, work and Marg Foggerty's letter. Bones were an undesired extra.

'The bones might never have been found if it hadn't been for the blood on the grass,' said Father. In his heart he blamed

Charmian Daniels for the discovery. 'Could have rested there for ever otherwise.' He wished they had; his CID unit already had three major crimes to investigate: the murder of Nella Fisher, the shooting of Sergeant Margery Foggerty and the theft of the illustrious emeralds. He did not need some long-dead male to put a name to.

Although it was true that the theft of the Duchess's jewels (mainly hers, but oddly enough the Duke had lost almost as much – Father owned no jewellery himself, not even a cufflink) had been handed over to a Metropolitan specialist team, he had been obliged to offer back-up help. Thus he had lost Sergeant Bister, who, while still giving nominal assistance to the local investigation, was happily assisting in the hunt for the lost necklace, tiara, and brooch, the full parure, in short, as he was learning to call it.

'Pity Marg didn't get round to finishing her letter,' said Elman, probing his boss a bit. 'Might have helped.'

'Possibly.' Father thought she'd written enough and wished she hadn't written as much as she had done. She could have left him out.

'No idea, I suppose, of what she was going to say?'

'None.' Father stumped round the table and picked up his coat. 'Come on, Fred, you know what Marg was like. She put herself about a bit. After Bert took off. Went round all of us at one time.'

'Toned down a bit lately,' observed Elman.

'Agreed, but there it is. I don't know what she wanted to tell me. Don't think I've spoken to her for months.' Although they were about to have a talk on the matter of her possible bent behaviour. Possible? Now he knew about the flat in Spain and the money in Jersey, there was no doubt. 'But I'm sorry she had to go in that particular sort of way.' Murdered, he meant, but wouldn't say the word. He had liked her, hadn't been able to help it. But that was long ago.

He put on his coat. 'I'm off. Keep me posted.'

'Will do.'

'I'm going to the opera tonight, on Sunday too. Charity do, y'see,' he said gloomily. 'Black tie and all. Not my style but the wife wants it. Smart occasion and all that. Everyone there.'

Elman was sympathetic, knowing that Ellen Father nourished social ambitions and that Father tried hard to keep her happy.

'You'll enjoy it,' he said, 'when you get there.'

'Want to bet?' and the Chief Inspector departed with slow steps. Father was overworked and under pressure and getting too much media attention, and somehow for this too he blamed Charmian Daniels. She always seemed to pick up publicity.

This was not how Charmian saw it. She had observed her photograph in the daily papers without pleasure. One and all they had used the same snap as Nella had had pinned to her wall. It might be the only one they had, or it might be that someone had got wind of its appearance in the Fisher case, you could never be sure with the press, they could be devious. Or it might just be coincidence.

But as with Inspector Elman, she did not like coincidences and she was not pleased to be splashed on the front pages with the headlines that she had discovered a body. Not even true. She had found some blood which led to the discovery of a body, and then some bones.

The bones had no connection with the death of Margery Foggerty and Nella Fisher, as far as could be established, but Margery and Nella had been killed by the same gun. At the moment no one knew whose hand had pulled the trigger but it was a fair assumption that same hand had caused both deaths.

The good thing was that Kate was no longer a suspect. Instead, her father had stepped into her place.

He was being quietly hunted through all his usual haunts but so far without result. Either his friends and drinking companions were very loyal or they knew nothing. A surveillance was kept on Wellington Yard, which infuriated Annie who could observe the watch from her windows.

Charmian had several heavy days of work in London, which inexplicably raised her mood and made her feel better.

To cheer up Kate and her mother, Charmian had invited them both to a concert performance of *Ariadne auf Naxos* in the Castle. The Waterloo Chamber was full, but when Charmian had finished looking at an elegant portrait, painted by Sir Thomas Lawrence, of one of the conquerors of Napoleon (she thought it was the Prince Regent himself, who had certainly never been on the field of Waterloo but had nourished the fantasy that he had fought there), she turned her head to see Dolly and George Rewley sitting across the aisle.

Dolly gave her a self-conscious smile.

'I didn't know George was coming tonight,' whispered Kate. 'He didn't say he'd asked Dolly.'

'Dolly may have asked him.' If so, naughty Dolly, she thought. Weren't you going to leave Kate and George to each other?

'Mmm.' Kate did not sound convinced.

'Don't let it spoil the evening.' Charmian repressed a slight smile. Much as she loved her Kate, it might not do the girl any harm to realise that George Rewley was not her sole property. She was inclined to regard her men as parcels to pick up and put down as she pleased.

On her left, Annie looked up from reading the programme. 'Who's the man?'

'Which one?'

'You know the one I mean. Across the aisle.'

Charmian told her.

'Ah,' Annie nodded. 'He's that one.' The orchestra had finished tuning up and was preparing itself for the overture. 'Dolly I know, of course. Attractive girl, isn't she?'

'Very.' Dolly looked blooming tonight in a vivid red dress.

'Also a copper. Do you think they are here to watch us?'

'No.' Charmian shook her head. 'Don't be paranoid, Annie.'

Annie looked unconvinced. Like daughter, like mother, thought Charmian. Quite naturally, they thought of themselves at the centre of the stage.

'Not everything is about you. This is an evening out, Annie,' she said firmly. 'Enjoy it.' She needed to enjoy it herself, the appointment with the specialist was coming up fast and she was nervous. She feared the surgeon's probe. Not because of the pain, there wouldn't be any, it was just a look-round, no knife, no stitches, but for the feeling of invasion.

Also, there had been someone in her garden last night. A rosebush had been torn up and thrown out into the road.

Another invasion.

All three women were uneasily aware that many eyes were

on them. Charmian Daniels was a public figure, and Annie was known to many because of her distinction as an artist, she was famous in her way. Kate had a lot of young friends. So they couldn't hide. As a group, Charmian thought, they were brave to come out together. She saw Annie put her chin up and concentrate on the music.

Bravo, Annie, she thought. I hope Jack deserves you. But certainly I do not deserve him. She had kept from Annie the news of Jack's violent appearance in her life. There are things you cannot say to friends.

The overture finished, and Ariadne paced her lonely island. A woman deserted by her lover. Too late, Charmian remembered the plot. She glanced at Annie who appeared perfectly calm; she was able to separate art and reality.

The opera is short, although the part of Ariadne is an exacting one. Richard Strauss had no mercy on his performers. But Helena Asherton, a young singer, triumphantly delivered her two exhausting arias, one after the other, and at last was carried up to Olympus by Bacchus in a chariot of stars.

Well, it might suit some women, Charmian decided, as she came down to earth herself after the soaring music, but possibly not me. Heaven, for me, does not mean transportation by a god-man.

She leaned across the aisle and spoke to George Rewley. 'I've got a table for dinner in the Donjon. Join us.'

George hesitated. 'I'm not sure.'

'Oh come on, we won't discuss the case.' Or cases.

The Donjon in St Julien's Tower had been converted into a restaurant for the benefit of the concert audience, and if you stayed eating long enough then you might see the performers come in for supper.

Charmian had procured a large round table in the middle of the room. Everyone else had to pass them to get to their tables, so there were plenty of greetings. Annie was taking it well, smiling at her friends, and Kate was rising to her feet to hug and congratulate Helena Asherton. They had been at school together, but Helena had pursued her career with rather more single-minded devotion than had Kate.

'Join us, Helena. There is room, isn't there, Charmian?'

126

'Of course.'

But Helena had her own circle of fellow performers to eat with and after a shy confession that she would be singing the same role at Glyndebourne this summer, she moved off to another part of the room.

'I wonder she can even talk after those two arias,' said Kate.

'Yes, it is hard on the voice. But I expect she knows how to protect it.'

Over the cold chicken in cream and garlic sauce, Dolly said to Kate: 'I didn't know I was coming till the last minute.'

'Oh?' Kate's eyes flicked towards George Rewley who was talking away happily to Annie.

'My mother meant to come with her new husband, but he had to fly off to Strasbourg so she sent me the tickets. I didn't want to sit on my own so George obliged me by coming. He knows more about Richard Strauss than I do.'

The promise of not talking about the case was kept through the first two courses of the meal, but while waiting for coffee they began. Annie started it.

'Come on, we can't not talk about it. Be unnatural. I know you are looking for my husband,' she gave George Rewley a hostile stare. 'You're all after him. Come to that, I'm looking for him myself. Jack, come home!' She drained her glass and filled it up again.

'Watch it, Annie,' warned her daughter. When Annie drank it was always wine and she could drink too much.

'Well, that's how it seems to me.' A little belligerency was creeping in.

George Rewley kept silent, well aware of the difficulty of his position. A detective in love with the daughter of a suspect. But he was encouraged by the look in Kate's eyes. He could read a promise in them.

'I agree with Annie,' said Dolly Barstow suddenly. 'We should talk about it. We're all in it together.'

The trouble with working in a relatively small community was that inevitably you got to know some of the actors in a crime. If Dolly looked around the room she could see a man who had been involved in a fraud case and been lucky not to go to prison. There was Freda X, better not name her and she wasn't

127

really Freda, who had been running a call-girl service and gone to prison, only to emerge better dressed and more prosperous than ever. Dolly could only speculate what the new business venture was but it was said to involve Japanese money. And serving at table was a waitress who had probably poisoned her lover. He was a chef in the restaurant where she had worked. Not dead, of course, but he had had an uncomfortable day or two.

No, Dolly thought, she knew too much about everybody. Mind you, everyone was here tonight. Present also at the concert and now dining in the same room were Lady Belvedere, widow of a famous general, Biddy Maincox, straight out of her TV soap rehearsal and a variety of City magnates with their spouses.

A crowd of new arrivals was just being seated across the way. Among them Charmian saw CI Father in company with a pretty, sturdily built woman in a strapless dress. He'd seen Charmian and her table of friends but was pretending not, he probably was not pleased.

'The second Mrs Father,' whispered Dolly in her ear.

'What happened to the first?'

'Couldn't stand the life. Went on a Caribbean cruise and never came back.'

The waiter brought a large pot of coffee and put a dish of chocolates in front of Charmian. Across the way CI Father was frowningly trying his cold cucumber soup; he stirred it doubtfully. Soup ought to be hot, not cold, and it should be brown or red in colour, not pale green.

Charmian took a chocolate. 'All right,' she said, giving way to the silent pressure. 'Let's talk. I'll begin. It's like a plant, this case is growing.'

'You can say that again.' Annie reached for her wineglass which was empty and she looked around crossly.

'And it is doing so in well defined stages,' said Charmian. She did not pass the wine to Annie. 'The first stage was when the girl Nella Fisher arrived with the story of threats to Dolly and Kate.'

'We know a bit more about her state of mind now,' said Dolly.

'True,' said Charmian, remembering her trip to the Fisher family in Cheasey. 'I think she wanted money and didn't mind how she got it. But the threats she came out with, the story of a policewoman who was hated and threatened, and whom Dolly identified with herself, were not imaginary. Some muddled truth lay behind them.'

'We all agree about that,' said George Rewley.

'Nella herself named Jack Cooper, how seriously, we don't know, but she was aware that Kate had money.' Charmian turned towards Dolly. 'But, at that time, although she was keeping quiet about it, Dolly had seen something that made her look at Sergeant Foggerty herself as a suspect.'

Dolly nodded.

'So that was stage one. I was in the US at the time and knew nothing about it. Then Nella herself was killed. Not a policewoman, not Kate or Dolly, but the girl. That was just about the time I returned.' Charmian looked at the faces round the table. 'Am I getting the stages right?'

'Absolutely.' Dolly spoke up in clear voice.

'When Dolly told me about seeing Sergeant Foggerty with Jake Henley in Cheasey, I started to look at her seriously as a suspect. Foggerty came forward with a story of seeing Nella with her killer that could be interpreted as a confession.'

'It could have been,' said Dolly. 'Seemed to be so to me.'

'So we come to stage three. Foggerty herself is killed with the gun that killed Nella Fisher. And we find a skeleton.'

'You'll never find out who that is,' said Annie. 'A visitor from Outer Space, I say. Came to visit our planet and fell into a hole and got buried.'

'I daresay identification will be difficult,' agreed Charmian.

'A male, in his early twenties, cause of death unknown, but I think we might get somewhere,' said Rewley. 'He wore a red wig. The remains of it were there in the earth. He may have been bald. I think that should help, don't you?'

'Well,' began Charmian doubtfully. If it was a good wig, who would know what was underneath?

'And the little finger was one joint short on each hand. Can't be many of those around, can there?'

'So what's happening?'

'The skull and the hands are going to an expert in London – the best for the job. She is going to reconstruct the face and the hands to see if anyone recognises him.'

'Plus a red wig?'

'Plus a red wig,' said George.

Life was a kind of circus sometimes, and he could never decide whether the victim or the police were the clowns.

The Forensic team had mentioned to him one other little puzzle about the bones, but had nothing definite yet. He decided not to mention it.

'Let's call the skeleton stage three-and-a-half. And there may be no connection with the deaths of Nella or Marg Foggerty. Except that the blood led the way.' Charmian looked around the table. 'Have I left anything out?'

'I know you don't like me here, listening to all this,' said Annie, still aggressive. 'But I will speak up.'

'Since you started the whole discussion, why not?' asked Charmian.

'I don't think you are paying enough attention to Jake Henley.'

'I don't know what his motive for a double murder would be.'

'He's a criminal,' said Annie doggedly.

'Even criminals need a motive.'

'He doesn't. Not that one. From what I've heard, he likes violence. And he hates women.'

'He's certainly not my favourite man,' admitted Charmian. 'But he can't be arrested just for that. It's been tried and they had to let him go.' Not for the first time, Jake Henley was walking free. What they needed, and did not have, was hard evidence. 'A few facts are what is wanted.' She looked towards George Rewley.

'Before Tom Bister went off to look for the missing emeralds, he told me that he had so far got no positive leads from Forensics on the house in Merrywick Parade,' said Rewley briefly. 'If it was Henley he would be far too spry to leave any traces. And if he sent a contract killer the same applies.'

He sat silent for a moment, then said:

'But I don't believe it was Henley. He's a pro. Marg Foggerty was obviously about to leave the country, the sensible thing would be to let her go. No need to kill her. And I certainly don't see him writing 'women' in blood on the table. He wouldn't bother.'

You haven't seen Henley's face when he's in a rage, thought Charmian.

'Forensics take time,' she observed.

'Agreed. And anything could turn up. We'll have to wait for it . . . ' He hesitated. He had had a bit of information that very evening and perhaps now was the time to pass it on. 'One thing . . . the blood in which the word 'women' was written was not Marg Foggerty's.'

'So it has to be the murderer's blood?'

George Rewley hesitated. His friend in the laboratory had laughed when he had passed on the information, but now did not seem the time to share the full joke. If joke it was. 'It's not Jake Henley's blood,' he said carefully. 'His blood group is known and it is not his.'

'And the blood on the grass?'

'Not Foggerty's either.'

'Another someone from Outer Space,' said Annie, rising to her feet. 'I'm off home to see if hubby's back.'

'I'll take you,' said Kate.

'I'm walking,' said Annie. 'Can do and will.'

As they all strolled towards the door, George said: 'Oh and there's a message on its way to you about that bottle labelled Vitriol. It's not vitriol.'

'Never thought it was.'

'No, it's a mixture of mineral oil and synthetic yellow colouring. Banana, I believe. You can buy the oil in any chemists and the colouring in any grocers.'

'Doesn't sound like Henley, does it?'

'No, he'd go for the real stuff.'

Charmian started towards her car which was parked carefully under a light. She was always careful these days.

'I'll walk with Annie,' called Kate. 'See you tomorrow, George.'

'Right.'

Charmian approached her car. George Rewley came with her in a polite way. 'Something I wanted to tell you. Better not said in front of anyone else. Marg Foggerty was writing a letter when she was interrupted. She tucked it under a blotter. We

131

found it. It may have been why she was killed. She started a letter to CI Father. I'm not sure if it was going to be a confession. But it would have been a tale. She began: I have something to tell you, Tony.'

'She called him Tony?'

'Apparently.'

Charmian stood still, thinking. The castle loomed above her, its walls silvered in the moonlight, so remote and old you could expect to see the ghost of old mad King George III looking down at you and still mourning the loss of his American colonies. 'No disrespect to Tony. I suppose she had known him a long time. But it's interesting. He knows, I suppose?'

'Yes, sure. Not many other people do, though.'

'Any chance he could guess what the story or confession was going to be?'

Rewley shook his head. 'No. I haven't heard a word. But I wouldn't.' He was checking underneath her car. 'I hope you do this regularly yourself? Don't want you blown up.' He straightened up. 'No, you're all clear.'

'Thank you, George.' She started the car.

'I'm thinking of getting a bike myself. You can't plant a bomb on that so easily.' He added: 'I hear you've had a call from Vander?'

'Yes. Know him, do you?'

'Not to say know. Who does?' George chuckled. 'I've heard his work is so sensitive that he doesn't even use his real name. He's not called Vander at all. Come on, Dolly. Thanks for dinner. My turn next, I've got a new recipe.' George was an accomplished and ambitious cook.

They said goodnight, and Rewley came round to the door of Charmian's car to close it. Common courtesy, she thought. But he had something more to say.

'About the blood. It's a bit more complicated than I said, and it's confidential. Not human blood at all. Animal blood. Not sure yet, what kind.'

As she drove down Maid of Honour Row, Charmian noticed a car parked by her house. She drove past, studying it. Any sign of anything suspicious and she would drive on.

But Sergeant Vander got out of the car and identified himself.

'Do you have a dog, ma'am?'

'Yes, a Labrador.'

'Golden? Quite small for the breed?'

'Yes, but doesn't live with me all the time, only some weekends. He lives with a neighbour. A friend, Birdie. What's happened?'

'A woman out walking a dog was attacked tonight in this road. She was hit from behind. She may have been mistaken for you. The dog was your dog.'

Birdie, thought Charmian. My friend and neighbour.

# CHAPTER THIRTEEN

## *Monday, October 16, to the early morning of Friday, October 20*

Charmian hurried to see her old friend, Winifred Eagle, in hospital. She had been unsure at first whether it was Winifred or Birdie Peacock who had been attacked, but a little thought had convinced her that Winifred was the woman who would be walking Benjy late at night. Winifred was the bolder spirit of the two.

These two ladies were well known locally for various activities, ranging from supporting an Indigent Cats' Shelter to organising a circle of white witches, although this latter organisation was in abeyance at the moment. Birdie was also something of a healer, while Winifred felt homeopathy was the better bet. They could both be relied on to offer advice and assistance to those in need, and even to those who were not. They were kind, energetic, helpful and meddlesome. But they were a package deal, you had to take them whole or not at all. Benjy loved them, as did Charmian, although she kept a weather eye open for trouble: she had seen them through various alarms and disasters, ranging from arson to murder and sexual harassment. Winifred had done the harassing. She had a powerful and not too carefully suppressed sex drive, surprising in a lady of her age and genteel appearance. 'I don't like men,' she once confessed to Charmian, 'so much as need them. Only one at a time, of course.' But even this statement was delivered in a doubting voice, as if she might, one day, experiment on a larger scale.

Accordingly, she was not surprised to be visiting Winifred Eagle in hospital. It could have been prison. But she was anxious.

Winifred was in a small room in the George V Hospital. She was lying flat on her back with her head heavily bandaged. One eye looked bruised but she was talking away in a loud voice. Birdie sat by her bed; she was doing the listening, which was often Birdie's fate when in company with her friend and landlady.

'How are you, Winnie?' asked Charmian.

'Oh it's you. Come round this side, I can't raise my head. Move out of the way, Birdie.' Birdie obediently stood aside. 'You ought to be here instead of me, you know.'

'Should I, Winnie?' She had thought that herself. Straight away.

'I went into your house to get Benjy's drops.' Benjy was taking a hormone prescription to promote his development, he had given them a little worry that way. 'Doesn't know if he's a dog or bitch,' Winnie had said trenchantly. 'Came on to rain while I was inside, borrowed your mac, that old red one, knew you wouldn't mind.'

'No, of course not,' said Charmian.

'Walked down to the cricket pitch, let Benjy run – he's improving on those drops, by the way, he's coming down nicely now – trotted back, hurried down the Row. It was raining heavily by then and I had my head bent. Mistake that, should have been looking, because I got bashed on the head. From behind.'

'Oh Winnie.'

'Not meant for me. His mistake. Thought it was you.'

'I'm afraid so. I am sorry, Winnie, dear.'

'Any idea why? I mean, I think I have a right to know why I was nearly done in.'

She had almost been killed. Charmian had spoken to the doctor before entering the room and it was clear that the blow had been hard and fierce. Only the fact that Winifred must have moved at the last moment had saved her.

'Came very close,' said Winnie; her voice was getting weaker but her temper remained fierce enough. 'If Benjy hadn't barked I would have been a goner. He chased right down the road, bless him.'

'I don't know why you were attacked, but I'm attending to it.'

'Oh thanks.' In a sardonic voice.

135

Birdie said anxiously: 'Don't work yourself up, Win.'

Winifred was her mentor as well as her landlady. They had been friends since girlhood and Winifred had always known best. Been the strong one. Birdie didn't want to be left alone. Winifred must not die.

'I won't go, old girl,' said Winifred. 'Not this time, anyway.'

'Benjy's doing quite well. I've got him in the car outside. He wanted to come in but I had to say no. They do let dogs in some wards.' The geriatric ward, but Birdie would not mention that. 'As comforters.'

'Why not here then?'

'You're in Neurology.' Charmian spoke up. 'It has to be kept sterile.'

'You're trying to frighten me, I'm not brain damaged.'

'No,' said Charmian soberly. But she nearly had been. The doctor had let her know that. Another fraction of an inch would have done it and the brain damage would have been mortal.

'But I've got a terrible headache and they won't give me anything for it. Or not yet.'

'They're coming,' said Birdie. 'Sister said so. On the way.'

'It's my head.' The one unbruised eye was able to express what Winifred felt well enough. 'The raincoat's done for, though. Blood all over it.'

A nurse appeared at the door with the drug trolley. Winifred's long-awaited medication was about to be administered.

'I'm afraid you two must go now,' said the nurse.

Charmian leaned over. 'Win, before I go, anything you can tell me about your attacker? Anything you remember? It was a man, I suppose.'

'I don't know, I didn't see. Ask Benjy, he was looking and went chasing off after him.'

'He was a brave boy,' said Birdie. 'But I thought we'd lost him. Didn't come back till late. Still, he was noble.'

'Yes, but useless.' It was a true judgement of Benjy and the way he always was. He tried but never succeeded.

'You two ladies must go now,' said the nurse, shaking out a tablet or two.

'There is something,' said Winifred. 'He smelled of cigar smoke. I remember that.'

As they left the room, they heard her protesting vigorously that she wanted a homeopathic remedy, or at the very least a natural herbal painkiller like feverfew, and to take those capsules away.

Two days passed, three days. Normal working days in London, home to Windsor in the evening. Winnie Eagle was making a good recovery and was likely to be let out of hospital soon. The search for her attacker was going on, but so far to no avail. In the Incident Room at River Walk the investigation into the deaths of Nella Fisher and Margery Foggerty was grinding on, but if Elman and Father had any fresh leads, they were not saying. As far as Charmian was concerned, all was silence. Still, three days was nothing in an affair of this sort.

All this time a quiet surveillance was kept on Charmian's house in Maid of Honour Row, yet each day there was nothing for Sergeant Vander to report. No one was seen.

Not even Jack Cooper. Least of all Jack, who was sought but not found. They had tracked him to the house of one companion but he was gone. The friend's wife had come home and turned him out. Where he had gone no one knew.

On the fourth day, Charmian kept her appointment with her specialist.

Dr Evans, who was a pretty, plump young woman, was kind to her. It was part of her job to be gentle to frightened ladies and she was exceedingly good at it. She had been frightened herself at least once which shaped her attitude. When you had worried yourself sick (and you a doctor) because there was blood where no blood should be, you knew how to respect another woman's fears. Men could only guess, some might do it well, others much less so. Might not even want to do it well. Some women had claimed that male surgeons chose a gynie specialty because they wanted to dominate women.

Marian Evans, whose mother had been a fan of George Eliot, knew exactly who Charmian was since she made it part of her task to find out what she could about the background of her patients. It all helped. She was building up her practice and meant to reach the top of her particular tree before she was forty. She had a few months left.

She summed up Charmian even as she took her first notes. She didn't make many notes because she had a hidden tape recorder which did the serious business for her, but a few notes reassured the patients.

Professional woman. Tense, nothing remarkable in that. Lost weight recently by her own admission and by the evidence of the waistband on her skirt. No serious weight loss, though. Fine face. Good bones. Expressive, thoughtful.

Hair and skin good. No sign of trouble there. You could tell a lot by a woman's hair. This one went to a first-class hairdresser too, and had been there recently.

Another excellent sign. Women were like dogs, really. Rough coat, rough hair, meant they were out of condition. Dr Evans had a Jack Russell bitch, who had just undergone artificial insemination, having been downright unwilling to couple with the chosen mate. Bitten him hard, in fact. Dr Evans meant to breed with her dog and then show the puppies. She would not deliver the litter, the vet could do that, there were limits. The bitch seemed in excellent health, but greatly to her surprise, Dr Evans was having morning sickness. You called that couvade, didn't you?

'Just go into an examination room. Nurse will help you slip into a robe.' And out of that nice-looking Missoni sweater and skirt.

Pretty woman, thought Charmian as she lay awaiting inspection in an apricot-pink shroud. Trustworthy.

Gentle too, she decided a few minutes later. Small deft hands. She looked at the ceiling and thought of other things.

As she got dressed again, she decided that wearing the blue, crimson and purple outfit had been exactly right, a heart-lifter. She heard Dr Evans murmuring softly on the telephone.

She emerged to receive the reassuring judgement that everything seemed as it should be, but perhaps an overnight stay to have a few more tests. Under a light anaesthetic.

So that was what the telephoning was all about. St Luke's Wing, the private side of a large London teaching hospital, one night, a week's time?

When Charmian went outside to claim her car, having paid a largish bill – it was pay-as you're-cured where Dr Evans practised, no running up of accounts – she found she had a parking ticket.

It looked like being an expensive business. She felt a flicker of envy for Winifred Eagle who was getting all this free.

When she got back to Windsor that evening, having put in a busy afternoon of routine work, there was a telephone call from George Rewley before she had even hung up her coat and spoken to the cat.

'Want to see something?' He sounded amused and alert. 'I think it might interest you.'

'Where?'

'On a table in the mortuary.'

No, thought Charmian, too much an echo of her day.

Rewley, who seemed able to read a person's thoughts even over the telephone and without seeing their face, spoke quickly. 'Don't worry. Nothing nasty, just bones.'

'Those bones?'

'Yes, those bones.'

'Are you suggesting I come down now?'

'Come and have a bite to eat with me and Kate and then I'll drive you over.'

Kate broke in: 'I second that. Bet you haven't eaten all day.'

'Not much.'

'Right. George will be over for you in ten minutes.'

'Make it fifteen. I want to shower, change and feed the cat.' Not in that order, though. Muff came first. She saw to that with a plaintive cry as of one long starved.

'Oh, just one more thing before I go, Muff.'

She dialled the number and waited for Birdie to answer. Birdie loved the telephone and never let it ring for long. Nor did she now. 'Birdie? Charmian speaking. How is Winnie? Is she home yet? Tomorrow. Oh good, I'll be round to see her.'

One victim saved from the Grim Reaper, anyway. Not everyone had been so lucky. Might not even be saved herself. No, mustn't have such a thought. Still, there it was . . .

But the idea did not stop her enjoying her meal with Kate and George. She felt very hungry as if she must eat to live.

Afterwards, she looked down at the mortuary tray on which the skeleton was laid out, all the bones neatly articulated.

The skull with empty eyes and nose, the jaws displaying the teeth. A good set, she noticed. The arms were stretched out along the ribcage and the legs extended.

She stared, then frowned.

'Notice anything?' asked Rewley.

Charmian turned back to look at the bones again.

'Small,' she said reflectively, as if recognising something special.

'You've hit it.' Rewley gave a brisk nod. The constables who had dug up the bones had commented with rough humour: bloody funny legs, this chap had.

Because she was still quiet, still thinking, he prodded a bit.

'Notice the legs?'

'They are very short. The trunk is normal size, the legs are not.' They were massive in roundness but stumpy.

'He was one of the Cheasey dwarfs,' said Rewley in triumph. He moved forward to touch the bones of the neck with a delicate finger. 'Strangled.' He touched the skull. 'Coshed on the head too. Probably unconscious when he was finished off.'

'They were such a decent lot,' said Charmian in a regretful voice. 'Kept out of trouble as a rule'.

'But by the very nature of the jobs they took, any one of them could come and go and not be missed. The circus, the racecourses, everyone would just assume they'd moved on. And they weren't very communicative as I remember.'

'That's true.'

'Once we start asking questions we will flush up an identity or two. Especially with the red wig and the short fingers as personal details. No, someone will give us a name. But isn't it interesting that it's Cheasey again?'

'No connection with Nella Fisher's murder, though.'

'Not that we know. And almost certainly nothing to do with Margery Foggerty's death either, but you never can tell for sure. Circles do touch.'

Charmian turned away. 'Poor little chap. Yes, he's a Tipper. That was the family name, wasn't it? Someone obviously hated him. Or feared him.' She watched as the mortuary officer slid

140

the bones away. 'I suppose you've told Elman and Father about this?'

'I don't think they're interested in this little chap.' He turned to the mortuary assistant. 'Thanks for showing us that, Pete. Who's be working on the bones?'

'Mr Ahab was. Not at the moment. He's on another body now.'

'Told you so. No interest,' said Rewley.

'But he's coming back to this one,' said Pete. 'He's got some problem with it.'

'Oh, what?'

'Some bone or the other, I think.'

George thought about this small but interesting fact (because Ahab was a very good worker) as he walked Charmian to her car. 'Elman and Father are grinding away at reading reports of interviews and checking contacts and background for Fisher and Foggerty. But their real interest is HRH's emeralds. They'd die to find them and beat the London mob to it. They wouldn't mind locating Jack Cooper, either. I think they'd settle for that at the moment. Kate pretends she doesn't mind, but she does, of course. It's making life a bit difficult for me and Kate at the moment.'

Charmian gave a sympathetic nod, but frankly, she thought, she wouldn't mind herself if Jack was safely tethered. He might not be a threat to her, but he might be. 'I'll look in on Annie,' she said. 'She may know more than's she's saying.'

'Kate says not. So does Elman. Reluctantly, because he thinks wives ought to know where their husbands are. Oh, and he's looking for a dead dog.'

'One that's lost a lot of blood?'

'Exactly. That blood had to come from somewhere. The dog had worms apparently. Seems you can tell from the blood.'

'Really?'

'Well, he or she was badly anaemic anyway. Even more so now, of course, if still alive. The dog might have an owner and the owner might lead to something. They're hoping. Frankly, they are waiting for something to turn up.'

'Aren't we all?' said Charmian.

They were waiting for something to turn up. It usually did in careful police detective work, and if it didn't then the case died on you.

You needed your bit of luck.

But the team down in the Incident Room on River Walk wouldn't be leaving it entirely to chance, as Charmian knew well enough; they would be using leg work.

She felt a pang. She had enjoyed that side of detective work, which was boring and tiring but also fascinating, enlivening and, in the end, invaluable.

She made a detour on her way home from the mortuary to drive past the Incident Room. A light still shone from one window, so someone was still at work.

She sat in the car outside her house for a moment before getting out. Check what you could see. Maid of Honour Row seemed quiet. A white van was parked at the corner of the road. It started up as she sat there and drove slowly past. In a little while some other suitable vehicle would take its place. Or a watcher might station himself in the trees across the road. She recognised the presence of her surveillance team and was glad of it.

When she got into the house, she telephoned Birdie again.

'Birdie, I forgot to ask: how is Benjy?'

'Oh very well. You can have him back for a few days if you like. Not for long because Winne will want to see him. Her little warrior, she calls him.'

'No holes in Benjy then?' She hardly knew why she asked. Of course there were no holes in Benjy. No one was after Benjy, it was another dog that had bled.

'Holes? Gracious, no. What a question. He was in a very excited state after he came back from chasing Winne's attacker, but he was not hurt.'

All the same, Charmian was irrationally relieved.

'If I thought he had been hurt it would have been off to the vet with him,' declared Birdie. She and Winnie might go in for homeopathy or even faith-healing for themselves but for their animals they believed in the best orthodox medical care that was available. In Windsor it was very available.

'I suppose there are a lot of vets in Windsor?' said Charmian. 'Who do we go to?'

'Mr George in Bassinet Street for dogs and Mrs Verney in Slough for cats. It's quite a drive but worth it, she's so good with the little creatures,' said the knowledgeable Birdie.

There were indeed many veterinary surgeons in Windsor and its neighbourhood and DC Thomas had visited half of them. DC Jimpson had been allotted the other half. The two young men had divided the task between them. One of them, Thomas, was a dog-lover; Jimpson was not and he was also allergic to fur and hair. He suffered. For two days they had been methodically calling at each surgery to see if a wounded, bloody animal had been brought in. They had got used to the smell of disinfectant and warm animals and learned to respect the vets.

Sneezing his way around, Jimpson felt he had performed above and beyond the call of duty. He had certainly visited Mr George. Mr George had been the one man to take pity on him and had recommended some medication, obtainable over the counter without a prescription, which would ease his allergy. After a few doses he would feel better.

Mr George had no other help to give: he had not attended a badly bleeding dog with worms nor had he any knowledge of one. He had sewn up one or two wounds – lacerations caused in fights – and set the leg of a dog hit by a car but that was about it. In any case, he knew all three animals well, had looked after them for years and none of his patients had worms. Wouldn't dare have, Jimpson felt.

By the end of the first day Jimpson had learned to appreciate one thing about the vets' surgeries; they were all staffed by personable young women in white coats with agreeable manners. By teatime he had drunk three cups of tea with fresh shortcake on the side and fixed up a date.

So he had a few good thoughts inside him when the two young men met in the evening to write reports and compare notes. DC Thomas was all but engaged to a WPC in Slough but he agreed, as a completely detached observer, of course, about the attractiveness of the young women who worked with animals. Animals definitely recruited a good-looking sort of girl.

But what information for the Incident Room had he come back with? Thomas cast his mind back to his first visit of the day – to the morning surgery of Jock Macgregor in Binns Street. Mr Macgregor was a tall Aberdonian who feared no animal. DC Thomas liked him and believed him when he said in a forthright way that any animal with a severe blood loss who came into his surgery would receive a transfusion at once and be admitted to his hospital. 'No, payment would not come into it. What was necessary would be done.' But Mr Macgregor would always be paid, thought DC Thomas, seeing his strong frame and well-muscled arms.

He added, equally forthrightly, that in his opinion DC Thomas should enquire of the District Cleansing and Street Cleaning Department because the dog was probably dead and cleared away by them.

'A stray, in all likelihood, ye ken, hit by a car and left to die.'

'We've checked there, sir,' said DC Thomas. 'And the police kennels where strays are sent.' He shook his head. 'Nothing.'

His second visit of the morning, this time to a very smart setup in the middle of a new block of flats where a sign directed him to the Animal Hospital, produced much the same results. Pretty girls in pale green overalls this time, and a bespectacled New Zealander in charge. The usual patient queue of owners was to be seen, plus pets on leads, in cages, or staring crossly out of padded wicker baskets.

And the answer was the same as with Mr Macgregor: no such dog has been treated here. But yes, if they did have such a patient, they would certainly get the owner's name and address.

He was discovering that animal health records are as carefully charted and kept as with the human animal.

So it went on throughout the day. A sense of monotony crept in and his feet ached. The more so as a lunch-time rendezvous with Jumbo revealed that both of them were getting the same result.

'Null and void,' Jimpson had said gloomily. 'That's what our work has been. We needn't have bothered.' The only good thing to come out of the morning was that he had a spray for his nose. At this point he had not yet met the young woman who was to catch his eye and provide another good point in the day.

'I don't know. Even a negative counts for something,' said DC Thomas. They parted to continue their round of visits.

Thomas plodded on, from address to address, making his careful enquiries and marvelling at the number of sick animals, but getting no leads in return.

The only memorable event occurred when he walked into a small, edge-of-town surgery where a cat fight of massive proportions had just erupted. Cats were hurtling from floor to window, and from floor to curtain, and from curtain to ceiling. Screams, hisses and low moans of anger echoed round the room about which fragments of fur were also flying. At first he thought about six cats were involved, but after a bit he saw there were only two, and small ones at that, one coal-black and the other striped in grey and brown. Various owners and surgery assistants were rushing about too, making as much noise as the pets, as they tried to separate them while busily blaming each other.

Thomas withdrew from the scene and decided to give that one a miss. No one had noticed him and he was grateful. That was a nasty scratch one of the owners had on her face, administered by her own cat too, judging by her reproachful wail. The cats, he suspected, were unhurt, all flying fur and shout and no real harm done. No one would ever blame the cats, he decided as he walked away, they were untrammelled, uncorrupted nature and no law could touch them.

Writing up his report that evening across the desk from Jimpson, he thought about the case. Since he was one of the police officers who had found Margery Foggerty and had known her slightly, he felt more involved with her murder than that of Nella Fisher where it had all started.

The bones he regarded as an odd freak, and one they could have done without.

Jimpson raised his head from his typewriter. 'Know what Elman and Father make of it? I heard Elman say that he fancies Jake Henley for both murders. Thinks it's his style. He used to keep pit bull terriers and might have one now. It's thought he does have. And with Henley you don't have to worry about motive. There'll be one somewhere. Doesn't have to be much with him.'

'What about the Coopers, father and daughter?'

'No, he's given up on them. But Cooper could have attacked the woman with the dog.' He did not think it likely himself, having once met Jack Cooper in a bar and thought him a decent chap.

'Those bloody dogs,' muttered Thomas, half to himself. 'Too many of them.'

'But no connection with the murders. That's how I see it. Just mistaken identity. Some personal feeling against Daniels.' He almost crossed himself as he used her name, having a wholesome respect for her, mingled with the notion that women shouldn't be in the Force and not so successful if they must be in it. 'Anyway, I'm making a prediction.'

'Which is?'

'Our next job will be in Cheasey, checking up to see if Jake Henley still keeps pit bull terriers and if one is injured.' Jimpson tidied his papers and stood up. 'I'm off, got a date.'

'I hate Cheasey,' said Thomas, as he went on working. He had finished the report due to go to Inspector Elman first thing the next day and was standing by the window when Charmian drove past. He saw the car, saw it slow down, and recognised her.

It was a small shock, seeing her, and he had an immediate reaction: Wonder what she's thinking?

An unknowable lady, he decided as he turned away. One who might well have enemies, inside and outside her working life.

That same evening, while the two young men were putting together their reports for Inspector Elman, and while Charmian and George Rewley were looking at bones, a small van had trundled into the Market Square behind the town hall. It was a neat yellow van with the letters W&SD displayed on the side.

This was the Windsor and Slough Dispensary for Sick Animals which arrived once a week. Set up by a daughter of Queen Victoria for the pets of poverty-stricken owners too poor to pay for treatment, it still survived, staffed by voluntary workers. There was no charge so you put what you could afford in the collecting box. Since it came into Windsor lateish in the evening it was convenient for those with a long working day, so a lot of people used it who could well have afforded an ordinary vet. Thus the collection box did well.

The vet in charge tonight was a young woman who was anxious for experience. She was packing up to go when a last customer arrived.

He was quite a sight. It was a wet night with a mist coming down, but he seemed overdressed even for a tropical downpour. A sort of uniform, she thought, possibly army uniform but with no insignia she recognised. Not that she would have recognised many, not being into the uniforms. A sort of greenish khaki. Over it the wearer had a thick overcoat, although it was a warmish night, and over the cap he had plastic protection. On a closer look she saw it was a shower cap.

She took her eyes off him to focus her gaze on the patient who was presented with an infected wound in the side.

'Nasty infection,' she said as she inspected it. 'Got a grip.'

'Been treating it myself,' muttered the man. He seemed peaceable enough behind his dark spectacles. Incognito, she decided.

'Should have brought her in before.' She was working on the wound. Her patient was a bitch.

'Didn't like to bring her out. She was in season.'

It was a very nasty wound. 'How did she get this?'

'I don't know.'

A lie, she thought, he must know. A deep graze. Looked like a bullet wound, she thought. Possibly she was being imaginative.

'Well, Major,' she said. 'You're in trouble. But I'll give her a shot of antibiotic, and you can keep up with antibiotic tablets. She might be in whelp by the way, Colonel.' Colonel. Give him the treatment. She noticed he had deposited a great swinging waterproof cape by the door, nearly blocking the entrance. She'd seen such a garment in war films on TV. Probably he was an actor. And then, of course, she knew there were types that liked dressing up and acting out themes. Displaced sex, in her liberated opinion. But she said nothing, not her place and anyway she was too busy with the bitch.

Folded money was placed in the collection box, but he got away without leaving a name or an address.

* * *

Charmian went to bed and slept with Muff by her side. The soft rain ceased, but it became very misty. As dawn came, Maid of Honour Row was obscured by the mist, with the houses at the end of the Row almost disappearing from view. A thick grey curtain hung over roofs and treetops. Most of the inhabitants were asleep but Muff had taken a trip through the cat flap, then returned rapidly. Not fit for a dog out there.

In the car, the man on guard over Charmian had his eyes closed as if asleep. His head rolled forward. Presently, he slipped sideways.

A circle of fire ignited with a puff around the front of Charmian's house. Soon it was blazing, licking at the window . and the door.

# CHAPTER FOURTEEN

## *The morning of Friday, October 20*

Charmian was woken by the smell of burning and smoke. She was awake and coughing before she realised what was happening to her. Once awake, her reflexes were fast.

She grabbed Muff and a coat and was down the stairs, putting on her coat and slippers as she ran. Muff hooked her claws into her shoulder and hung on. She knew danger when she smelled it.

The front door defeated Charmian, it was already alight. She ran to the back where a flame showed itself at the window. There was smoke coming through the door and the key felt hot as she got her hand on it, but it turned and the door opened.

She smelled petrol and burning wood, but she was through. She threw herself on the damp grass and drew in great lungfuls of air. She was still coughing and gasping when she realised that her right hand was sore where a blister was already forming. She examined herself carefully. No other damage as far as she could see. Muff had disappeared into the bushes.

She was supposed to be under protection, but the protection had failed.

Gathering herself together, Charmian walked round the side of the house, thankful that she was at the end of the Row. The fire had no hold yet on this far side. The smell of petrol was much stronger as she got to the front of the house.

No doubt about it, this fire was no accident.

The glass cracked explosively in a ground-floor window as she ran down the garden path. A van was parked across the road, but there was no movement from it. But the windscreen was shattered.

She pulled open the car door and the driver slipped towards her, headfirst. There was blood on his face from a wound in the eye.

The watcher had not watched himself; the guardian had been felled.

She heard the fire engines arriving at that moment. Somehow, someone had alerted them.

'It was me,' said Birdie. 'Or rather Benjy, he woke me up barking. Good boy.'

Charmian sat at the kitchen table in her friends' house. She was wearing a dressing gown belonging to her hostess; it was made of pale frilled silk, something of a revelation about Birdie's taste, and she was drinking hot tea. Muff had arrived unannounced and was receiving succour in the shape of a saucer of warm milk.

'Watched from the bushes and followed you round,' said Birdie knowledgeably, topping up her supply. She was usually more at home with animals than people.

'I'm glad Benjy barked.'

'Yes, isn't he a clever dog? So I dialled 999 and said FIRE. Then I came round. You were out cold on the pavement. I thought you were dead.'

'Shock,' said Charmian who was ashamed of herself for fainting. Not professional, she ought to be above that sort of thing.

'But you'd got out of the house, that was the main thing.'

'If it hadn't been for you and Benjy, my place would be a cinder by now.'

'The firemen were very good, but I'm afraid the ground floor will be very wet and smoky.'

'It's insured,' said Charmian absently. Her fire seemed the least of it now.

'And that poor man.' Birdie gave Charmian a sharp look. But she did not get an answer. 'Mustn't ask questions, I suppose.'

'I don't have any answers. Not at the moment. I'm asking questions myself.'

150

'Let me pour some more tea,' said Birdie, administering the only form of comfort she had to hand.

'I must get some clothes on. I can go back to the house, the stairs are all right and the fire never touched the upper floor.' Everything would smell of smoke, though.

'You can't live there. You must stay here, dear.'

Charmian stood up. 'Thanks, Birdie, but I won't bother you. Winnie will be back soon and you only have the two bedrooms. Keep an eye on Muff for me though, will you, please?'

'Of course, but are you sure about yourself, dear?' asked Birdie wistfully. She loved a crowded house, it was so cosy. Also, there would be plenty to talk about with all this going on.

'Quite sure, but thanks. I'll probably find a place in London.'

Fond as she was of Winnie and Birdie, she did not fancy being their guest. Apart from anything else, their housekeeping and cuisine was of an eccentric nature, depending almost entirely on their interests of the moment. Recently it had been organic vegetarianism. It seemed to involve a good deal of dust about the house. Perhaps that was growing organically too.

She could stay with Kate, or even Dolly, although it might be better to be independent from both of them while this investigation went on. Come to think of it, she had the key to Humphrey's London pied-à-terre. It was tiny but very central and would do.

The telephone rang while she was still standing there.

'It'll be for you,' said Birdie, not rising.

'May not be.'

'All the other calls have been.' And it was true that the telephone had been ringing almost continually since Charmian had arrived in the house. First a senior fire brigade officer telling her that the fire had been caused deliberately and that there would be an investigation; she could go back into the house, with one of his officers, but had better not stay there. Then the local police, then the local police, headquarters division, again. There was a lot to say.

She picked up the telephone. It was Annie. 'How did you know where to find me?'

Annie did not answer that question, she never bothered with inessentials. 'Come and stay here. You must.'

'George Rewley and Kate, I suppose,' said Charmian, answering her own query. 'No, I can't stay with you, Annie.'

'Why not?'

'Because.'

'Jack, I suppose? He didn't set fire to your house. He's calmed down now anyway.'

'How do you know?'

'Because I know my Jack. He always calms down. Anyway, I know where he is and he couldn't have been out burning your house.'

'What makes you so sure?'

'Because he's here with me and we were in bed together last night,' said Annie defiantly.

Charmian paused. 'Are you telling me the truth?'

'Would I lie?'

'No,' she said slowly in reply. 'I don't think you would, Annie. But I won't come. Have you told the police that you've got Jack with you?'

'Of course not.'

'I'll give you the rest of the day, Annie, for you to tell them, and then I'll do it.'

She put the receiver down before Annie could huff and puff.

The next call was from Kate, also offering hospitablity. But she refused this too.

'Thank you, and I appreciate the offer, but I have to refuse.' Surely Kate could see that it wouldn't do.

'I'm worried about you, Godmother.'

'I'm taking care.'

'Well, do that. I love you.' There was a little catch in Kate's voice. 'And what's more, I need you around. That fire, how could it happen?'

Reading between the lines it was clear, Charmian thought, that Kate did not know about the man who had been shot while watching over her. George Rewley, if he knew, had been discreet.

Dolly telephoned next, likewise anxious to help, but she was more worldly-wise. 'I know you can't stay here with me, wouldn't do, what with one thing and another, but my mother has a flat in Richmond that's not in use at the moment. She'd be delighted for you to occupy it. Quite secret and all that.'

It sounded as though Dolly had heard about the shot officer. She might not know all the details but she had picked up enough to alarm her.

'I think I'm fixed up,' said Charmian evasively. She had made up her mind to hide out in Humphrey's London flat, but the fewer people who knew the exact address the better. In any case, Sergeant Vander might have something to say on the subject. A so-called 'safe house'? She would resist that suggestion from him. Get in one of those and you could take some time getting out.

Under supervision from a uniformed constable on duty at her house, she collected some clothes, packed a case, and managed to get dressed.

A quick look round had revealed her sitting room and kitchen, indeed the whole ground floor, to have a thoroughly trampled-upon air. Might be the firefighters, might be Father and Elman's lot, but she guessed she could blame Vander for most of it. Looking for clues. He must be very angry.

The clues would all be outside, surely? No one had got inside. But as she walked down the garden path, she observed that Vander and Co. had been at work there too: the rosebushes had trampled circles around them.

'Bet you didn't find much,' she muttered to herself.

The constable met her with a message. 'Inspector Elman would be glad if you would call in at River Walk, ma'am,' he said politely. He picked up her case. 'Can I take this for you, ma'am?'

'Thank you, the garage is round the back.'

'There's no petrol round there, all clean, ma'am, we've checked.'

'Good.'

'The message from Inspector Elman was that if it wasn't convenient for you to go to River Walk, then he would call on you when it suited. I can put a message through for you.'

'No need. I'm on my way.'

She drove herself, the suitcase packed for London in the back of the car. She had filled in the intervening few minutes with a brisk telephone call on the car phone to her London office. Reassurance and calming words were necessary there because the media were already showing a keen interest in her welfare.

An actual press presence in Maid of Honour Row was prevented by a police barrier at each end of the road, but beyond it she spotted a clump of hopeful reporters lying in wait. She drove past at speed.

It was a short journey to River Walk, but the drive seemed to clear her mind. The threat to her was much more vicious and determined than she had believed at first. She had always taken it seriously but not been alarmed. Now she was concerned, because she guessed how much she was hated.

It was direct and personal.

But who hated her with such venom?

If not Jack, then whom? Somehow it felt like a threat emanating from Cheasey. Probably had Jake Henley's face on it which made a thought with teeth in it.

She had walked into something nasty and it had stuck like dog dirt.

Not at all to her surprise, Sergeant Vander was there in the Incident Room in River Walk, waiting for her. He was talking to Elman and Father, a conversation that was suspended as soon as she arrived.

Coffee was poured out, hot for once, and strong. 'Come on, sit down,' said Elman. Father pulled out a chair. To her fury, she recognised they were being masculine and protective.

Even more to her irritation, she also recognised that she was comforted by it. She wanted to be looked after. Never admit it, though, she advised herself. She took the coffee (welcome after dear Birdie's herbal tea) and put on a resolute face.

'Something to tell you. The Ballistics have done a quick job on the bullet that killed the DC in the van. The first tests indicate that it came from the same gun that killed Marg Foggerty. And Nella Fisher.'

This is where we came in, thought Charmian.

The three cases had become one. Only the bones remained, doing their separate dance.

## CHAPTER FIFTEEN

# Friday, October 20, to
# Tuesday, October 24

'I'm afraid someone is out to get you,' said Chief Inspector Father. 'And we haven't been very much good to you.'

'It looks to me that I may have been the destined victim all the time: that it was me Nella Fisher heard threats about, and not Dolly Barstow, nor even Margery Foggerty. They just got in the way.'

'That's putting it bluntly,' said Father.

'I feel blunt.'

Sergeant Vander remained professionally cheerful and practical.

'Where will you be staying? I can fix you up with somewhere safe. You've made your own arrangements?' Perhaps he was not so pleased with that news but the smile stayed on his face. 'London? Right, you'll let me know where?'

Charmian thought she would but was not prepared to say anything at the moment. She had to get into the flat to begin with, and only then would she pass on the address to a strictly limited circle.

'I'll let you have all the details next week.'

'Right,' he said, still cheerful, more so if possible. He seemed to flourish on disaster. 'You can disappear. Go missing. No one will know where you are.'

'So we hope,' said Elman to whom gloom was a more natural medium.

'And the man who was shot dead? Has he left a widow and a family?' His fate troubled her, he had died on her account.

Vander said: 'He was unmarried.'

'How did he die?'

'Shot through the windscreen. In the eye.'

'Poor devil.'

'Yes,' said Elman heavily. 'It's not what I like to see happening on my patch.'

'There'll be a man on duty all the time at your place in Maid of Honour Row,' said Vander. 'And I'm getting it fixed up. Windows boarded and that sort of thing.'

'Ask them to look out for my cat.' Birdie had promised to heed after Muff and her needs, but there was no doubt that the inquisitive cat would go back for a look-round at her home.

'Will do.'

The relentless cheerfulness of Vander was beginning to irritate her. 'As soon as it's ready, I shall go back.' She knew he did not want to hear this.

'I don't know if that's wise. He'll try again.' He frowned, then bounced back. 'Still, it'll take him a bit of time to set up anything again. So you ought to be all right for a bit.' He looked thoughtful. 'I'd give you three days anyway.'

Did he really say that in all seriousness, Charmian asked herself. Or was it his idea of a joke?

One day, two days, three days.

'We'll lay hands on Jake Henley somehow. It's him, I'm sure of it. Got his name on,' said Father. 'We're not talking about motive: we're talking about someone who likes to kill.'

On the same day as this meeting, there was a discovery in Merrywick.

In Merrywick the streets were swept and cleansed once a week, which was not so often as had once been the case, nor so often as they needed, but better than many places achieved. The inhabitants of Merrywick paid a high community charge and were an exceedingly vocal group, well able to shout for their rights and to object to sweet wrappings, empty plastic food containers and battered lager cans in the gutter. Consequently they were provided with a road cleaner, an old-fashioned figure with a broom and bag-on-wheels. On the day after the fire in Maid of Honour Row he arrived with his apparatus in the Dulcet

Square and Dulcet Road area of Merrywick. He went to Dulcet Road first, because it was Dulcet Road's turn to get cleaned and he was a methodical worker. Besides, he liked Dulcet Road, a pretty, neat street, one of his favourite work areas, nice lot of folk in Dulcet Road, not mean with their possessions. He had found a nearly full bottle of wine in a bin there once.

He was a benign man who took his work slowly and calmly. Dirt would always be here, you only moved it around. When he came next week the same layer of paper and plastic would greet him. Looked the same, could be the same, except he knew he had shifted last week's burden. He had once found a dead bird, that had been his most exciting moment, but even the feathered corpse had not moved him greatly. A dead baby now, he thought as he swept the gutter, that would be something.

One of the jobs he performed with mild interest, because there might be a baby there, was to empty the rubbish bins which were placed by a hopeful Refuse and Cleansing Department at various appropriate spots on the street. Although they were capacious, they were rarely full. Most people who had tried for virtue at all seemed to deposit their rubbish around the bin rather than in it, as if they had reached towards it with closed eyes.

'Just not looking,' muttered the street-sweeper. The least censorious of men (because he did recognise that if it wasn't for dirty people he would not have a job), he gave them a mark for trying.

He started to investigate the bin where he could see something interesting wedged. A big, bulky something. Not a body certainly, which was just as well because he regarded anything he found as a perk of the job and a body, except as something to think about, he did not want.

He put in his hand and dragged out a great heavy cape made of some oiled and shiny fabric.

Army issue, he decided knowledgeably. Keep out anything, that would, from water to poison gas.

Army issue, last great war or possibly Korea. It looked a mite old-fashioned, he didn't think the troops wore anything exactly like it now. All dressed in white, weren't they, against flash burns? Or was that the last video he had seen?

'Surplus army issue,' he said aloud, as he shook the garment out. It was quite serviceable, with no holes and not torn anywhere. His eyes traced some dark stains on it. Great areas of stain.

Blood.

'That's why it's been dumped,' he muttered. 'Someone's had a nasty accident in it and doesn't fancy it any more. But it's useable.'

Accordingly, he rolled it up, not without difficulty, then he stowed it away in his container in a private place of his own. It would wash.

He was not planning to wash it himself, of course. He handed it over to his wife when he got home.

'Got stained with something.' Better not mention blood, women were funny about blood. 'Give it a sluice down.'

Busy with serving the meal, she barely glanced at it. 'Put it in the shed outside if it's mucky, I'll do it later.'

She had too much to do the next day because of a wedding in the family to bother with washing anything, but the day after that she remembered it and went out to take a look.

In the daylight, spread out in the garden, she did not like what she saw. 'That's blood. I'm not going to touch that, he can do it himself.' So she returned the bloody cape to the garden shed.

In the evening, she said: 'You do the washing, Jim. I don't fancy it.' Easily, not a man to stir himself unduly, he agreed to do it when he had time. No hurry there.

Several days passed. One day, two days, three days. The family wedding was comfortably over.

She was more of a newspaper reader than her husband. She saved up the papers and read them as a batch on Sundays. She said you got more of a story that way.

She read the gossip columns first, then her horoscope (which was sometimes in arrears, as it were, so she could check if it was right), then the criminal cases. She liked a good murder. The sports and financial pages never.

She finished her reading for the week, then made a pot of tea. You thought better over a cup of tea.

This time it took three cups before she came to a decision. The cape had better be delivered to the police, and if Jim wouldn't take it, then she would do so herself.

It might be quite a nice trip, she liked a policeman. It was the uniform. She'd always been a girl for a uniform. Not tomorrow though, she was having a perm tomorrow.

She'd had a boyfriend who was a PC when she was sixteen, he'd done well and risen high. She didn't think she'd bother Jim; she would walk into the nearest police station and ask for Tony Father. Her hair would be looking nice too.

Charmian also had an appointment to keep. Not with the hairdresser, that would come afterwards, but with a doctor and a hospital. Only an overnight stay, she had been informed, and she should be out the next day.

The word 'out' evoked unpleasant thoughts of prison.

But you're safe in hospital, she told herself. No one can get at you there. Except those licensed to do so, of course. But the thought itself told her how frightened she was.

She had informed Sergeant Vander of her London address: 20A Moneypenny Road, Knightsbridge, Humphrey's flat, but she had the uneasy feeling that he knew already and also who owned the lease.

'Don't expect to find me there much,' she warned him. 'But there is an answering machine.'

'I'll keep you up to date with things, ma'am. I'll be seeing Elman today.'

He had nothing much to report, but what he knew, he told her. Cheasey was being searched for Jake Henley. He had certainly been there, been seen in The Grey Man, but at the moment he was not to be found.

'But a man like that can't hide for long. He'll burst out, it's his nature. And then we'll have him.'

One small new piece of information he did have, however. It was a negative fact: Jake Henley had once owned several pit bull terriers, he was suspected of organising dog fights. But these animals had been put down after police enquiries. He had been seen with a greyhound in the last year, but it had not been around recently. In spite of being a dog owner, he did not have the reputation of being a dog-lover.

Sergeant Vander was also a man who did not like animals, and he felt that this might be one point of contact with Jake Henley.

'Have you got any idea what he might have against you, ma'am?'

'No,' said Charmian. 'Except that I once gave evidence against a porn ring he was involved in.' She had not forgotten the photograph of herself in Nella Fisher's room in Cheasey, which must have some relevance somewhere. Unless Nella Fisher had liked her face. 'For him that would be enough. If it is him.'

'Elman seems convinced. I'm open-minded myself.' He remembered something. 'Oh, ma'am. You'll be glad to know that Jack Cooper has returned home. His wife reported him back. He's down at the station being interviewed, so Elman tells me. But it looks as though he's in the clear about the attack last night.'

'Thank you.' So Annie had done the right thing. She always did in the end, wise, bold, loyal Annie. But there was no denying that, as a family, the Coopers made mettlesome friends. Yet you didn't stop loving people because they were trouble.

She hadn't told Annie where she was, nor Dolly, nor Kate. For a few days they would have to wonder.

She made some necessary arrangements with her London office, spent an uneasy day, and then disappeared into the hospital.

She felt a little triumph that she had kept this fact from Sergeant Vander. You had to have a few secrets.

No one knew where she was.

## CHAPTER SIXTEEN

# *Tuesday, October 24, to Wednesday, October 25*

And yet Dolly Barstow got through to her. Charmian was sitting by her bed in the small, pleasant room allotted to her in the hospital when the telephone rang beside her.

'Charmian, Dolly here.'

'How did you know where I was?'

'George Rewley told me. He seemed to know. Why didn't you let me know too? How are you?'

'I didn't tell George and I'd like to know how he found out. I wanted it kept quiet. And I'm all right. This is just a check-up. I'm in for a new job, as I expect you know, and a clean bill of health is looked for.' This was the line she had decided to take if she had to talk about the affair.

Dolly accepted this statement without argument but not without a small inner query.

'And I shall be out tomorrow. So stop worrying.'

'That isn't why I rang. Listen, they've picked up Jake Henley. A contact of Elman's turned him in. He's in custody.'

One up for orthodox police work then.

'You'll find lots of messages on your answering machine, but I thought you'd be glad to know tonight.'

'I am.'

'Of course, he's not admitting anything. But he wouldn't.' Dolly sounded confident.

Dolly knew where she was, George Rewley knew where she was. Probably Sergeant Vander had found out. It was, after all, his job to know, and he had put Dolly on to tell her the news about Henley.

'And look after yourself.'

Charmian was in the private wing of an old-established London teaching hospital. Her room had a certain austerity to it but she had been provided with a charming nurse who looked in with a menu so that she could choose what to eat.

'Can't guarantee you'll get it, mind you,' she said cheerfully. 'They do have lapses, but I'll do my best.'

'Fish, I think, in a cheese sauce. Sounds good,' said Charmian, not feeling hungry.

Charmian ate a modest supper, but refused the sleeping tablet offered to ensure her a good night's rest before tomorrow's activity. She had plenty to think about; sleep did not seem to matter.

She was glad Jake Henley was back in custody. He was a dangerous man, given to irrational and wanton violence. If he had a pain inside him, he saw to it that the world shared it.

It might be that he had killed three times in fits of irritation . . . his victims had got in his way or represented a threat of some sort.

'We aren't looking for a motive,' Father had said. 'With him you don't need one.'

Lying back in the hard hospital bed, she studied the shadows on the ceiling (you were never absolutely in the dark in this place) and put together a profile of the killer.

The killer was quick and neat in the execution of his task. He did not draw back because of a bit of blood, perhaps he even liked it. The murders gave no evidence of any great preplanning so they may have been spur-of-the-moment jobs. He must have known Foggerty because she let him into the house. Almost certainly knew Nella Fisher too. What was the relationship there? Worth thinking about. His third victim he had not known but he had blocked the way to his most hated object: Charmian Daniels.

She summed him up: a man who used violence easily, who left few clues, not as if careful planning had gone into his crimes but as if it was his very nature to be anonymous; he slid through her life unnoticed. Or wearing a mask.

162

A man who lived on his own, and did not have a regular job. Or was self-employed.

As she tried fitting Jake Henley's face (you could certainly call him self-employed) into this profile, it became one of the shadows on the ceiling as she fell asleep.

Anonymity, she thought, was not Jake Henley's style. No one could call him faceless.

Next day, while she slept under anaesthesia, Jake Henley sat in his cell which he shared with another man whom he despised. He made the position clear and the man was hunched up on his bunk keeping his feet well out of the way.

Henley had put up with one night inside a police cell in the Alexandria Road station without doing much sleeping.

His mind went back in a pleased way to his brush with Inspector Elman as he had arrived. He knew Elman of old, and knew that Elman had been glad to haul him in. Had enjoyed doing it a bit roughly. But he'd got his own back. Elman was a dressy man and had paid for it.

Elman had brushed the marks of Jake's hands off his suede jacket in some anger. There were fingerprints on the pale skin. 'If you've damaged this I'll sue you for it. I paid three hundred for it.'

'You were done. That's a bit of old horse, not proper suede. I've got a better one than that I feed the pigs in. I'll give it to you; I feel generous.'

'I don't want anything from you, Henley, but I'm going to see you get something. I promise, and with luck it'll be a nice long stretch. A lifer, I wouldn't wonder. Say more than one, a triple stretch to keep you banged up till your balls drop off.'

'You're not supposed to talk to me like that. Where's my solicitor?'

Elman shrugged. 'It's a bit late to get him out tonight. He's not at home.'

'He's got an answerphone.'

'He's not answering his answerphone.'

'And you wouldn't get a message to him tonight if he was. Don't tell me, I know your tricks.'

'No tricks.'

'That scraggy cow, she's behind this, isn't she?'

Elman had said nothing.

'I hear she's coming here, in your patch. A boss figure, eh? You'll have to pull your forelock to her, won't you?'

'You know more than I do.'

'I've got my sources of information. You tell me, and I can tell you more.'

'Good for you.'

'You won't keep me here, I can tell you that for nothing, I'm clean.'

'Like the lily, I suppose? Lock him up.' Elman strode away.

I won that one, thought Henley. And I'll win the next one. I have a friend here. He thought back with satisfaction to a face he had seen on his way in. The face had aged a bit but the hair was still red. Dyed maybe. The thought of a cop with dyed hair gave him great pleasure.

In the late afternoon of that day, Charmian had packed her bags, put on her grey suit with the matching cashmere sweater that was a kind of uniform for her at the moment, and paid her bill. She too was clean or so they had told her.

As she walked out of the hospital, she heard fire alarms ringing. No one seemed to be taking any notice, but suddenly the carpark was full of fire engines.

She sat in her car thinking about it, then she picked up the telephone and got through to Sergeant Vander.

'I'm in the carpark of the InterCollegiate Hospital in Histon Street, just off the Strand.' The private wing overlooked the river.

'Yes, ma'am.' He tried to sound surprised but did not quite manage it.

'As I came out I heard the fire alarm start ringing. All things considered I am wondering if it was anything to do with my stay there.'

'Stay where you are, while I check. I'll ring back.'

His tacit admission that he had known of her movements had registered with Charmian.

In a surprisingly short time, he was ringing back. 'No, not a crisis. Just smoke from a badly adjusted boiler. It set the alarms going and they always send a fleet of engines to a hospital just in case. Obliged to do it.'

'Thanks for finding out.'

'No problem. All well, ma'am?'

'Everything is absolutely dandy. Thank you.'

Black mark to you there, Vander, he said to himself, you should have kept your mouth shut.

She sat where she was for a minute or so more, thinking over the interview with her doctor which had had some prickly moments. One, anyway.

More than a prickle, she thought, more like a dig with a knife. She still felt sick with the pain of it. Emotional pain can be worse than the physical sort, no anaesthesia there.

Marian Evans, her doctor, had a sweet face, looked a bit tired, she decided, but after all the woman had been operating for about twelve hours. Her little investigation into Charmian had been a minor episode in the day's work. She must have had other major operations to perform. But she had had all her attention focused on Charmian.

'I'd like you to stay another night, really.'

'I want to get home.'

'Well, take things quietly for a bit. An anaesthetic is a powerful blow to the brain, however carefully administered.' She looked down at her notes, shuffling the pages. 'You will be glad to know that you ought to have no further trouble. We've tidied you up.'

Charmian gave her a wary look. 'Oh?'

'Yes, at some stage you appear to have had a spontaneous abortion.'

Not spontaneous, Charmian thought, but carefully arranged. Almost certainly her doctor knew this and was simply being tactful. After all, it had been some time ago, but legal even then.

'It was not quite thorough, a little . . . ' she hesitated, looking for the right word, 'a little bundle of tissue remained. Quite . . . ' She tried to find the right word, 'quite petrified, of course.'

Charmian stared at her. 'Tell me.'

In her gentle voice, the doctor said: 'The pregnancy looks as though it was of two embryos.'

Twins, in short. One disposed of, one hanging on. Not macerated, not chewed up by the body's own processes, but staying around. Not growing and developing either, just steadily withering away into a nothing.

'I didn't know it was possible.'

'It happens sometimes. It was giving you trouble.' She shook her head. 'It was causing the bleeding. I dealt with it. You shouldn't have any more bother now.' The papers were shuffled gently again, the interview was over, it was time to go. She was an ex-patient. Treated. Cured. Bother eliminated.

Bother seemed the wrong word for what had gone on. Too trivial. There had been an important event in her body in the past of which she had not realised the full significance.

I am ashamed, she told herself. This feeling inside me is a deep shame. I wasn't ashamed when I had the abortion, it seemed the right thing to do, but I feel shame now. No, perhaps not shame. Retrospective grief for what might have been.

What to do now, she asked herself, as she started the car. Go home and get on with life.

I didn't check underneath the car before I started it, she thought. But it must be all right, because here I am, moving through the traffic.

Abstracted. She was in Windsor and driving towards Maid of Honour Row before she remembered that she couldn't live there now and that she had her stuff in the flat in London.

She sat in her car for a moment, wondering what to do. Then she drove on to her own house, impelled by a strong need to be there.

The signs of fire still stood out around the windows and front door. The windows had been boarded up. But the fabric of the house was undamaged. She could live in it. She *would* live in it.

Then the front door opened and Kate, followed by George Rewley, came out and walked down the garden path. They were as surprised to find her as she was to come across them.

'You're not supposed to be here,' said Kate. She opened the car door and stood looking at Charmian.

'And what about you?'

'Someone has to see about getting the repairs under way.

Redecoration too. The upstairs is a bit kippered. I suppose you were insured? And George is the official police presence without which I would not have been allowed in.' She gave him a friendly smile.

'I'm glad to see you, Kate,' said Charmian soberly. And looking so much yourself, she thought. The strained, wild air that had marked Kate earlier this season had vanished. She and George seemed at ease with each other.

'And I'm glad to see you too. You look so much better.'

'So you do,' agreed George.

And suddenly, it was true. Charmian felt a surge of life and energy. She got out of her car, feeling free and cheerful. The right hormones were moving into action.

'You can't stay here,' said Kate.

'No.' Charmian gazed at the front of her house. 'But I'll just take a look round. Where's the cat?'

'With Birdie and the dog. She says they are getting on together and not fighting.'

'It's never the dog,' said Charmian. 'Always Muff.' The cat was better at it too, a born scrapper, whereas Benjy liked to take life quietly and gently, annoying no one. He came from a long line of distinguished gun dogs, but he was no sportsman. By temperament he would have run with the fox rather than hunted with the hounds.

Kate and George Rewley told Charmian to watch out for the floorboards in the hall as they had been taken up to check on the wiring. Which was all right, she would be glad to hear, so the electrics were useable. If she was determined to go in, that is. They were on their way home, then going to a concert.

'How's Dolly?' she called after them.

'Working hard,' George called back.

Once inside the house she could see that a start on tidying after the fire had already been made. The kitchen had been cleaned, with china and cooking pots bright and cleansed.

All over the house the curtains had been taken down and had disappeared, presumably to be cleaned. She could detect Kate's hand in all this.

She opened drawers and cupboards to investigate her clothes, but having been protected they did not smell of smoke. Well, not too badly. She moved her clothes along the rail to inspect and check.

No, nothing in here needed to be sent away. She might rinse through one or two of the shirts and blouses just to be sure. She didn't want to sit next to someone at a meeting or a committee and smell of smoke. She held a silk shirt to her nose. No, sweet and fresh. She kept lavender bags on the hangers, which helped.

In front of her was the outfit, no longer in its first use but still nice looking, which had figured in the photograph on Nella Fisher's wall.

She closed the door on the clothes. She thought of all the things that had happened to her in those clothes, some good, some bad. That had been quite a case.

If she had made an enemy in any case, that would be the one to do it. Jake Henley had been involved, but he had not gone to prison. However, his profits from his criminal enterprises had certainly been slashed for a period. Perhaps more importantly, he had lost face.

She had clipped his wings and insulted him at the same time. She remembered some of the things she had said.

She could not remember the exact words she had used but contempt certainly came into it and other things besides. The newspapers had edited out some of her crisper phrases in their reports of the case.

Of course, a lot of other people had been involved as well, a whole host of minor parasites and hangers-on ranging from the photographers who took the pictures to the people who let their premises be used for the sessions.

As she left the house, she thought about Nella Fisher. If Nella had had that photograph on her wall, then she had known of Charmian and who she was. She must have had a pretty good idea that Charmian was the real person under threat from Jake Henley. Not Dolly Barstow, not Kate.

But she had put on a show, told a lot of different stories. Well, possibly she had had hopes of getting money out of Kate. As she nearly had done. Kate would probably have come across if Nella had not got killed first.

Charmian unlocked her car. Nella was a confused kid, it

looks clear to you now, she told herself, but that's hindsight. Not the same for her, maybe, you had to allow for human blindness. And heaven knows the girl had had reason not to see events clearly.

Charmian started the car. She had to decide where to go now. Back to London?

Unpredictably (she must be more tired than she had thought) she found herself driving past the Incident Room in River Walk. The windows were dark. Not much, if anything, going on there tonight. After all, they had Jake Henley.

Without thinking very much about it, she turned the car round and drove back to Maid of Honour Row. She unlocked the door of her house and went in. She'd take that job on offer here. It went without saying now, the decision had made itself.

She made up her bed with fresh linen, undressed and curled up comfortably.

It was good to be home.

# CHAPTER SEVENTEEN

## *Thursday, October 26*

The next morning, while Charmian was driving off to London, planning a full day of normal work, the street-sweeper's wife waited for her husband to go off to work, then she put on her coat and packed a parcel wrapped first in plastic and then in newspaper. She made a neat job of it and it fitted on top of her bicycle so that she could push it round to the nearest police station and hand it in, as was her plan.

She had read in the paper about the murders in Merrywick and thought she knew her duty. The rain cape might have something to do with the deaths so she must let the police have it. In any case, she didn't want to keep it a minute longer. It was an unholy object in her opinion and made her skin creep.

She had given up the idea of taking it to Chief Inspector Father, about whom she had made a few enquiries. Now she knew his rank he seemed too grand for her to call on as a friend, and a mere forgotten bit of his past she would not be. But she had a more personal and feminine reason for avoiding him: she had put on weight and her hair was grey. There were more than a few wrinkles as well. She was no longer the pretty, flighty blonde piece he had known.

Better let that girl rest in peace and not be dug up with a start of surprise. Or worse, he might not recognise her at all.

But she had remembered a young policewoman called Barstow who had been very kind over a little matter of a shop-lifting charge of which she had definitely not been guilty, although the magistrates had been hard to convince. Dolly Barstow had been understanding then and could be counted upon, she thought, to be helpful now.

Besides, she was performing a public service in returning what might be vital evidence in a murder case.

All the same, she felt jumpy as she approached the Alexandra Road police station. Not a place with happy memories. She slowed down to a crawl as she approached.

To her great relief she saw Sergeant Barstow herself in the process of parking her car. With a tentative, nervous smile, she approached to do her duty.

'Hello, love,' she said, putting her hand trustingly on Dolly's arm. 'I've got something to show you.' She started to fumble at the parcel on the front of her bike.

'What is it?' Dolly looked at her. 'It's Mrs Arthur, isn't it?'

'That's right.' She had the parcel open now. 'Here it is. It's a rain cape. Army stuff, I think. My husband found it in a bin in Merrywick.'

'So?'

Mrs Arthur was pulling at her exhibit. 'I read the papers; I know about the murders. I think it's evidence.' She pointed. 'Look at this blood.'

Dolly opened her mouth to say: If it's evidence then don't touch it. But she reflected that if it had been in a bin and been removed by Mr Arthur and packed up by Mrs Arthur, then it was probably too late to worry about fingerprints. Forensic traces would have survived.

'But it's this I didn't like,' said Mrs Arthur. She was pointing to a stained patch of dried blood to which were stuck a few strands of ginger and white hair. 'That's dog. Dog hair.'

'Right. Come on then, bring it with you and come with me. You'll have to make a statement.'

'What, me?' Mrs Arthur started to pull away. 'No, no not me. I don't want to make a statement.'

Dolly took her arm. 'Come on, I'll look after you. You've got to do it.' And your husband too, she told herself, but I'll break that to you later.

The vet from the Windsor and Slough Dispensary for sick animals also read the papers. Not as regularly as Mrs Arthur, but with much the same technique: she saved them up in a pile and got at them when she had time. On the same day that Mrs Arthur pushed her bundle up the hill to Alexandria Road police station, the vet finished her stint of reading for the week.

'Better do something about this dog,' she said to herself, reaching for the telephone. Unlike Mrs Arthur she had no intention of appearing personally.

She got through to the duty sergeant at Alexandria Road who put her through to Inspector Elman in the River Walk Incident Room. She could hear the buzz of activity in the background, but she got an attentive listener.

'Yeah, the dog was in a bad way. A bitch, actually . . . A nasty wound, gunshot, I thought, just a glancing blow, a flesh wound but it must have bled . . . The man? Well, it was a stinking wet night and he was all done up in rainclothes and a cap. Dark spectacles as well. I might recognise him.'

'Would you know the dog again?' asked Elman.

'Oh, I'd know the dog. Never forget a patient. If he's still got it.'

'What do you mean?'

'If he follows the treatment I laid out, then the dog should make a nice recovery. If he doesn't, it'll be dead.'

The two pieces of new information were absorbed by Inspector Elman, who was grateful enough. It was time for the case to move, and these two items might just be a sign that it was about to do so.

'Never rains but it pours,' he said. 'But still, you couldn't call this a downpour exactly, could you? Just a few helpful drops from which we might or might not get something.'

He sat back, and accepted a cup of coffee.

'So, we have a description of the man who is possibly the murderer of Marg Foggerty. Possibly. Then, just possibly again, we have the rain cape he wore.' He still thought it could have been Jake Henley all togged up like that.

The description of the man and the dog was circulated, while the cape was sent off for intensive study.

By this time both Inspector Elman and Chief Inspector Father knew that Charmian was back in residence in Maid of Honour

172

Row, having been informed of her return by Sergeant Vander.

'She shouldn't be there, and I don't want her there, but she is and we will have to wear it.' Vander added more cheerfully: 'Still, you've got Henley. Hang on to him, will you?'

'Yes,' agreed Elman. 'We're moving him today from Slough Road to a safer nick. Too many friends for comfort, that boyo.'

'Tell you what, you'd better do your best. Look after the lady. She's coming your way as a boss.'

'How do you know?' asked Elman suspiciously, well aware that Vander had sources of information denied to him. Rumours he had heard himself, but this sounded more definite.

'I can smell out that sort of thing,' said Vander.

'You look after her. It's your job.'

'I'll do my bit, if you'll do yours,' said Vander, not quite laughing.

Charmian was not told about the finding of the cape, or of the call from the vet, because there was nothing yet to tell about them.

In the early afternoon of that day, she went out shopping to buy something, anything, frivolous and feminine.

'As I am a woman, and not a substitute man,' she told herself, 'I shall behave like a woman and still do my job.'

She bought herself a red cashmere shawl, edged with fur. It was beautiful, expensive and probably of limited use, but it satisfied a hole inside her, like a cream cake or a rich chocolate might sometimes do.

On the way back to her office, she ran into a colleague. 'Celebrating the new job?' she was asked.

The name on the bag which contained her purchase was a giveaway. Browns.

'Just felt like it.'

'You won't find working down there like working in London,' said the colleague, who always knew the score. 'Living there, too. Might be a disadvantage.'

'I might move to live in London,' said Charmian defiantly.

'Of course, it's a plum job. And if a national detective force is formed, as looks likely, you'll be well in, nicely placed in a very good position.' A nod of the head. 'Yes, all in all, you've made

173

a good career move. You'll make enemies, but it'll be worth it. Probably.'

As she went into her office, to hide her purchase away from her secretary, Charmian recognised that she had been silently admitted to the bleeding company of career soldiers.

And as she drove home, the red cashmere draped across the seat next to her because she wanted to see it, she acknowledged a truth.

You did make enemies. She had made enemies, there was one outside looking for her now.

'Having an enemy' made it a very passive relationship, made you a victim.

Put it differently, she told herself: he is your enemy but you are his enemy. That was active. In other words, don't sit there waiting for your enemy to attack you, but go and get him. Of course, they had Jake Henley.

Not all the answers, though, and that concerned her. There never were all the answers in matters of this sort, although you wanted to know them.

She parked outside her house in Maid of Honour Row, observing with satisfaction that workmen and decorators had already been active. The windows and door had been restored to normal . . . Paint had been applied and a notice pointed out that it was still wet.

So she went in through the back door to the kitchen. Here there was still disorder but repair work was under way. But in a methodical thought-out kind of way. It all bore the mark of Kate.

She took herself and her possessions upstairs. On her bed was the cat Muff, who awoke and looked at her, mouthed a silent greeting, then went back to sleep.

She had been right to come home.

She had started to put together a scratch meal from oddments in the refrigerator when the telephone rang.

'You're back.' It was Sergeant Vander.

'You keep a sharp watch.'

'Not sharp enough.' There was a slight pause before he added: 'You're staying home tonight, ma'am.' It was more of a statement than a question.

174

'No,' said Charmian; she knew now what she was going to do. 'I think I want to take another look round the house where Nella Fisher lived, There's a question or two in my mind.' A silence followed, and into the silence she said: 'I shall need a key.'

Vander said: 'You'll have to get that from Elman. He wants a word with you anyway. I think you'll be hearing from him.'

Charmian put the telephone down. If it wasn't a ridiculous idea to have in connection with that man, she would have said he was embarrassed.

Pretty soon she knew why.

Elman rang. 'I hear you want to take a look where Fisher lived.'

'Is that all right?'

'Yes, I can let you have a key. The place is empty now, nothing to see that I know.'

'I'll collect the key.'

'Don't you bother. I'll send someone round.' He hesitated, then came out with it: 'I'm afraid we've lost Henley.'

'What do you mean?'

'He got away. We were transferring him from one place to another and he got away.'

Charmian controlled her emotions. These were so many and so diverse – anger, fear, outrage, surprise – that she managed a streak of sympathy for Elman. 'How did that happen?'

'I'm afraid he had help . . . A bad apple of our own. A chap we called Red Rick. He was under investigation. Or about to be. He covered for Henley.'

There was a short, awkward silence before he went on: 'So I'd rather you stayed home tonight, ma'am. Let me arrange for someone to take you round tomorrow.'

Was home safe then, and tomorrow a better day? 'All right, I won't go to Cheasey.'

'Thank you.' Elman sounded relieved.

Within ten minutes, and not meaning to be a liar, she was on her way to where Nella Fisher had lived. I'll just take a look round from outside. Stay in the car. I won't run a risk.

Behind her, the man placed on guard by Sergeant Vander followed at a discreet distance. 'Damn her, what's she up to?'

he asked himself as the traffic lights stopped him and she sped away. At the next junction, he lost her.

The quiet suburban road in the area which bounded on Slough, Merrywick and Cheasey was lined with cars so that she had the usual job of finding somewhere to park. The street was empty of people. All inside having a meal or watching television, she speculated; a major news story was breaking in Eastern Europe so perhaps it was the latter. Not everyone watched the television news or cared what happened, but there were one or two popular soap operas on the go at this time of the evening too, which were probably claiming an audience.

No one was around as she walked towards the house. She stood at the gate, studying it. Even from here you could tell the place was empty. Silly of her to come here. What was the point?

But something pulled her on. Just nosiness, probably. Or that instinct which had made her a good detective.

She walked up to the front of the house to stare in through the ground floor window. The young couple who had lived here had left it tidy. The place had been rented, part furnished, so the pair had taken what was theirs and left the few remaining pieces of furniture arranged in stiff order.

She walked round the side of the house. The garden looked neglected, but at some time someone had loved it because here were roses in plenty, and shrubs of hydrangeas and fuchsia. These had flowered, and no one had picked the flowers so that they hung dead and brown on the stems.

None of the curtains were drawn so she could see into the kitchen. She could also see that a small side window had not been properly closed; there was enough of a crack for her to be able to lever it open and get in.

She pulled at the window tentatively, not having any firm intention at that point. But the window gave a fraction. Just enough to let her squeeze her hand inside to pull the lever down and open it.

She was inside and standing on the kitchen floor before she thought twice about it.

The house smelled damp and unlived-in as she moved through it. She tried a switch but the electricity was off; however, she could see enough in the light from the streetlamps.

Nothing of interest on the ground floor, but she went upstairs to where Nella Fisher had lived. Nella, who was, one way and another, the start of this affair.

Nella's room smelled of disinfectant and kitchen soap as if someone had scrubbed it throughout. Poor Nella, not even a ghost could make headway against the smell of carbolic.

But there was no sense of a ghost here, Nella hadn't hung around. Her spirit, if she had left one behind, was probably back in the library at the local polytechnic, trying to locate a way forward in life. It was what she had always been trying for, only life itself had failed to co-operate.

The room was empty. Darker, too, than it need have been because a blind was drawn down over one window. Charmian raised it to let the light from the street outside reach the table by the bed.

The bed itself had been stripped and the mattress rolled up, but a few books and papers lay on the table.

Charmian flipped through the collection. A couple of blue Penguins of the sort familiar to all hard-up would-be intellectuals: one on withcraft, one on sleep, and another on the early Celts. All old, all second-hand, all well read. Underneath them were notes of some of the lectures Nella had attended.

Charmian read them quickly; they attested that Nella had not been a good notetaker.

Something fluttered out. A bit of newspaper. She picked it up, seeing at once that it was another copy of the photograph of herself. The one that had interested Nella so much that she had stuck it on the wall.

She took the cutting over to the window to look at it again. Wait a minute. Not just her photograph. Unconsciously, you always put yourself in the centre, the great old ego push, but there were other people in this picture too.

That was Jake Henley's profile, walking offstage. Quite right, he'd been involved in that case, been in court, walked out, free and pleased with himself, even if she had stung him with some of her comments. He'd got away with it again. You could see that in the cocky tilt of his head.

But in the background, staring straight at the camera, was the blurred face of another character.

177

I know that face, thought Charmian. By God, I do.

She tucked it in her pocket and made her way out to the car.

As she travelled through the streets, threading her way neatly through the traffic, the policeman whose duty it had been to protect her, and who had lost her, reported this loss to Sergeant Vander.

The news was transmitted to the Incident Room in River Walk, Merrywick, where an evening conference was taking place. They were all there: Chief Inspector Father, Inspector Elman, George Rewley and Dolly Barstow. Only Sergeant Vander had not yet arrived; he had many important responsibilities – Charmian was only one of them – and he delegated where he could. But he was in his car and travelling in a hurry towards River Walk. He no longer seemed so cheerful.

Elman groaned. 'What's she up to? Oh hell, she ought to be able to look after herself. We'll have to pray she can. Oh, we'll get Henley, I'm not worried about that. He can't get away far. Or for long.'

'About the bones,' said George Rewley. 'I think they might be helpful . . . '

The telephone rang, and Elman picked it up. He listened carefully, then replaced the receiver. 'Forget the bones for the moment. We've got something. There was a fingerprint on the bloody cape. And it matches a print found in Fisher's room. And it seems that under pressure DC Richards, our dear Red Rick, has come up with a suggestion.' He looked at them. 'We have a name.'

Charmian had a name, and an address also. She drove towards Merrywick, avoiding the street where Dolly Barstow and Kate Cooper lived, and passing the house where Marg Foggerty had died and the grassy, bloodstained stretch where the bones had been found.

She stopped outside the parade of shops in Merrywick. There was the house agents which had been involved in an earlier murder that had interested her. It had changed hands once again and had a new name, but it was open for business on this autumn evening although few people were buying houses this season. The

178

Indian restaurant next door was also open, but the dress shop further down was closed. The library had lighted windows and was doing a brisk business. The Keyright Employment Agency was open too. A woman was just leaving.

Charmian recognised her as Mrs Beadle, that well-known local inhabitant.

'Hello, Mrs Beadle,' she said as they passed. 'Looking for a job?'

'Not likely, not with him,' she tossed her head back to Edward Dick's establishment. 'Used to help his mother out sometimes, just as a friend, but he doesn't want me. Keeps half the place locked up. Always did, even when the old lady was alive. Not that she was herself for a long time before that. Bit senile, you know.' She was carrying a black plastic bag that was clearly too bulky for comfort. 'No, but I do his washing. Once a month.'

'It's too heavy for you.'

'Don't I know it. And I'm off to play bingo in Slough. Didn't want to take it but he insisted.'

'Put it in my car, I'll drop it in tomorrow,' said Charmian. She walked towards Keyright, and pushed open the door. The spaniel, Henry, who was crouched by the reception desk, where no receptionist sat, stood up nervously. He seemed to be the only one on duty.

'Mr Dick?'

Edward Dick, who had seen her coming and been waiting behind the door, hit her hard on the head; she fell forward.

When she came out of the darkness into the light again, bright, bright light was shining directly into her eyes. She closed her eyes. Then opened them again, memory flooding back.

She was looking at a white ceiling, she was flat on her back and she could not move. Her hands were crossed at the wrist and tied in front of her, her feet were tied together at the ankle.

She moved her head to study the room. She saw bleak, white walls, with two upright chairs against them the couch on which she lay, and a long table across the room. Nothing on the table. Blinds covered the one window and the bright lighting came from several spots, one focused directly and cruelly on her face. It was getting very hot. She was sweating. Then she became aware of her state.

She was naked, stripped bare.

A shudder started inside her and rippled outwards up and down her skin.

Edward Dick's face appeared from behind and hung over her. 'Well, here we are. Don't worry, we're quite private here. No one will see us.'

She answered something, but what it was did not seem to make sense. There was the word fool but whether she was the fool, or Eddie Dick, was not clear. She tried to sit up.

'Don't worry,' said Edward Dick again. 'I'm not going to rape you.' His face was quite serious, not a grin anywhere, but she was conscious he was laughing inside. 'That silly girl Fisher thought I was after sex with you. She didn't know me, but she deserved what she got. Nasty spying pig. Blackmail, if you please,' he laughed. 'It was a pleasure to shoot her. I'm a good shot. She hadn't got anything on me, though. I got into that house through a back window and took her papers. Such as they were. I needn't have killed her, really, and then Marg wouldn't have seen us together and I wouldn't have had to kill her either. Still, I don't know, it was coming on as a good idea. You couldn't trust her. Can't trust any woman.'

His breath smelled, Charmian thought. Anger gave her the strength to raise her head and shoulders. Eddie Dick moved round and appeared in front of her. He was carrying a camera towards a tripod.

'No, you're not to my taste at all. Dear old Marg was more my sort of girl, but I couldn't let her go on, more's the pity. She was unreliable, couldn't keep a still tongue in her head. She was a danger, poor cow.' He pushed Charmian back. 'I'm not going to eat you, either.'

But she had found her tongue. 'You're a fool.'

'Name me no names now.' He sounded blithe, as if nothing could touch him. With returning alertness, she wondered if he was high on something. Not alcohol, she could smell sourness but no drink, and he had certainly put his face close enough. 'Not exactly eat, just photograph, humiliate you . . . ' he liked that word so much he said it twice. 'Then kill you. I might put you in the river then. Or drive you out to the sea. I've got a little dinghy down at Shoreham. You might be in bits by that time, dear, but you won't mind. Not then. Earlier, perhaps it may hurt a bit. Hope so.'

He put his face almost against hers. 'I've wanted to hurt you for a long long time. I thought I had knocked your head off that night, but it was some other poor cow.' He was breathing heavily and gustily. 'Forget the fire, you ought to have burned in it, but you didn't. That was nothing, this is it.'

And you walked into it yourself, said a voice inside Charmian. You're the fool. She could feel the sweat running down her back.

'I've watched you strut around,' he said, 'and I've hated you and wanted . . . Got my phone calls, did you? So you knew it was coming . . . ' His own words seemed to confuse him, so he stopped and started again. 'I thought, I'll get you, you're the one. All women are the same, but you are the worst sort. You came into court and talked about porn and how evil it was and how people like me and Jake Henley were not men, not men at all.' He leaned forward and hammered on her shoulder. 'And I am a man, I am a man.'

Charmian kept quiet. A murderer and a porn merchant. He had dealt in porn from the Keyright Employment Agency. What better cover for people coming and going? Not only had he been well placed to deal in it at a high level, but placed as he was, with young people coming in all the time, he had probably been able to recruit subjects as well. Had he tried with Nella? She didn't have to ask why he had killed Nella: the girl had had a shot at blackmail and threats, poor child.

Charmian thought she understood about Marg Foggerty, too, now. Marg (had he admitted to some sexual relationship there? Better remember, just in case) had been going to tell what she knew about Nella's death and the whole dirty business with him and Jake Henley and the porn ring before clearing out herself.

Had Henley recruited Edward Dick? Or had they just naturally come each other's way as two dirty customers interested in the same trade?

Judging by the look of the room she was in, some of the

artwork had been done here too. The more clinical variety, not the sort that needed a homelike atmosphere.

She tried to relax, the thing was to calm him down, not to inflame him more. She seemed to have done a bit too much of that in her life already.

'Put your legs up. From the knee, Yes, like that.'

Let him photograph her in any position he liked. What the hell! If she survived, then she'd see to it that those pictures did not circulate. Do her no good at all. Even in this extremity, she could visualise the reaction of her male colleagues.

'Open them up. Wider now.'

And if she didn't survive? Well, she wouldn't be worrying about pictures then, either.

Wordlessly, she did what he asked. She could smell the thick odour of cigar smoke on his hands and in his hair. He had untied her legs so that she could part them, now he untied her wrists. She took a deep breath, but was careful to let her body stay limp like a doll. She closed her eyes, but inside, she was ready, waiting for the moment. I've got your laundry outside, Eddie Dick. There will be traces of blood on the clothes. I'll get you for Nella and Marg if I get out of here.

She was determined to get out.

'Let's do this,' he was muttering. 'Let's do this and this.' He was sinking deeper and deeper into his own fantasy, still photographing.

Then, from beneath the bench on which she was lying, a noise. A groan, a retching sound, and a sound of heaving sickness.

Edward Dick was checked. He stood still for a second. 'Trix!' he said. And in that second, Charmian threw herself at him.

She hit the bridge of his nose so that he screamed, and before the scream was fully out, she had kneed him in the groin. He grabbed at her but naked bodies have their own built-in slipperiness, and she had been sweating under the lights.

There was only one possible weapon in the room, and that was his camera. Charmian grabbed it and hit him on the temple with it, hard.

His foot slipped in the dog's sick and he fell to the ground, striking his head hard on the edge of the bench.

From underneath the bench, a furry ginger-and-white snout stuck out, and two anxious eyes looked at her. A great bandage covered the fur where a glancing bullet wound had bitten deep, but the dog had manged to work it loose so that it trailed from her like a train. She had been wounded when her master fired a shot at a woman she had seen but did not know, she had worms, and she was in pup. Of course she felt sick.

He's got two dogs, thought Charmian. Two bloody dogs and this is the one that got wounded when he killed Marg. Why didn't we realise you could have more than one dog?

It had been Trixie's blood on the grass, Trixie's blood he had used for the word WOMAN. She had been hit by a bullet meant for Marg Foggerty, going as his sad furry chaperone on that visit. Perhaps one of the dogs always went with him when he visited Foggerty dressed up in his gear. What a relationship.

He must have taken Trixie home over the grass because dogs need grass, not realising how profusely she had bled until he came out again with Henry.

Or perhaps he had thought that Marg had crawled out on to the grass, bleeding. No wonder he had looked upset that night. Charmian's stomach gave a heave of revulsion. She was in danger of being sick like the bitch.

'All right, Trixie,' she said. 'I might find a use for that bandage.' She looked round for her clothes.

She tied Edward Dick's hands and feet with the stained bandage and had just got herself into her dress when the first police car sent out by Inspector Elman drew up in the street outside.

# CHAPTER EIGHTEEN

## *Thursday, October 26,*
## *and afterwards*

She had some clothes on as the police team crowded in. Yes, that was good, but unfortunately the photographs had survived. There must be half-a-dozen or so, damn it. They had been collected and would be developed and produced as evidence.

She knew in her heart that, evidence or not, unprofessional conduct or not, she would have destroyed the photographs if she could have got to them in time. Any woman would.

But I am not ashamed of my body, she told herself fiercely. I will not let them force that kind of shame upon me.

'I wish I could have killed him.' She had not done so. Eddie Dick was unconscious but not dead. Not her fault, as it turned out. He had hit his head on the side of the bench as he fell to the ground. The police surgeon had pointed out the trianglar shape of the wound, and Forensics had found blood and skin on the corner of the bench. They would be able to tell the order of the blows too, no doubt, and work out which was the important one. Not that it mattered to her. He was laid out, and she was glad of it.

An animated group had assembled in the River Walk Incident Room. There was Sergeant Vander, newly arrived, who was angry. Charmian should not have been out on her own, 'on the loose' as he put it. Someone was going to be in trouble and it wouldn't be him if he could help it. Inspector Elman was on the telephone to Chief Inspector Father who had been called from an official dinner to hear the news of the arrest of Eddie Dick. Those two were quietly happy. The information about the photographs, so far undeveloped, was being discreetly handed over by Elman with an expressionless face that told all.

George Rewley was on another telephone talking to Dolly Barstow. She had news for him from Cheasey. He had asked her to ask some question for him, which she had done. She had then taken Mrs Henley, mother of Jake, to look at some remains.

In one corner of the room was the vet who had treated Dick's mongrel bitch. The animal had been brought round to the Incident Room by Charmian who felt she owed the creature something.

'Poor bitch.' The vet gave her patient a gentle pat on the head. 'Of course she felt sick, she's in pup. Fair-sized litter tucked away inside there. I'll take her with me. Come on, Trix.'

'What about the puppies?' asked Charmian nervously.

'Let you know,' the vet said as she left, the mongrel trotting happily by her side. Sanity had at last entered the dog's life and no animal had ever welcomed it more.

Charmian drank some coffee. She had tidied her hair, put on some fresh makeup and felt better, but what she wanted to do was go home and have a long hot bath in scented water. She needed cleaning.

But that was a wrong thought and she pushed it from her. I will not wear shame, she told herself.

Elman came over to her. 'Glad you picked up Dick's dirty clothes for the month. Forensics might get something from them. Traces to link him with Foggerty and Fisher. And there's the house, bound to be something there. His staff in the agency might have something to offer too. Must have noticed a bit.'

He was carefully not mentioning the photographs. But the news was out and running. It would spread through the masculine-oriented police world with the speed of light. Perhaps Charmian Daniels world turn down the offer of a job here? Maybe even resign and get out of police work altogether? There were certain things women could not take.

Elman went on: 'Dick belonged to a society that dresses up in World War Two uniform and acts out battles. He was sometimes General Eisenhower and sometimes Patton, old Blood and Guts himself. He fancied himself as the Americans, it seems. That's where he got the uniform cape. You buy them in special stores, the secretary of the society has just told me.' He was unsurprised at the variety and strangeness of human tastes. 'People,' he said, shaking his head. 'You off, ma'am?'

'I will be, when I've made my peace with Sergeant Vander. I'm afraid it's going to take some time for him to forgive me for shaking off his man.'

'Feels a fool,' said Elman blandly. 'No one likes that.'

'No.' Charmian met his gaze bravely. 'By the way, I am accepting an offer I've had to head a new unit in this Force. I shall be working here as one of you. Thought you'd like to know.' She knew the subtle damage the story of the photographs could do her, but her determination had hardened. She could fight for herself. And for the sake of the young ones coming up behind her, those like Dolly Barstow, she must do it.

'Glad to hear it, ma'am. I had heard rumours.'

'Of course you had. Well, I've accepted. It'll be official in the next few days. You can tell everyone.' At the door, she said: 'And I won't be sending out those photographs as Christmas cards.'

She knew she'd said the right thing. Shown she could make a joke of it.

To hell with the photographs. I will not be a page-three-girl boss.

George Rewley drove her back to Maid of Honour Row, since her own car was being held for a Forensic search. Just in case, she supposed, the bag containing Dick's laundry had deposited anything of interest on the upholstery.

'You'll get your car back tomorrow,' Rewley said, as if reading her thoughts, a process he was good at. 'I think Elman and Co. are just hanging on to it for the hell of it.'

'I got that impression too.'

'But I wanted a chance to talk to you. About the bones . . . I've been poking around and so has Dolly Barstow. And we picked up a story that interested us. One of the Tipper family, you remember, the little men, worked for Jake Henley for a while. He had lodgings in old Mrs Henley's house. There was a row of some sort and he moved away, or was thought to have done. I expect he couldn't stomach Jake and his ways, the Tippers were decent little men at base.'

'And you think this man is our skeleton?'

'The description fits. Especially the wig. But there's something else . . . ' he paused. 'The time Tipper took off was about the time Jake Henley's brother Gerry went missing.'

'You think perhaps Tipper knew something about that?'

'Or saw something,' said George significantly. 'Because there was one other thing: a couple of bones found didn't fit, so Mr Ahab said. They were extra. Human, but surplus to the requirements of the Tipper skeleton. Belonged to someone else. So we went down further. Dug lower still.'

Charmian waited. 'So?'

'There were other bones underneath. Another young man. The one had been buried on top of the other. I got Dolly Barstow to take Mrs Henley down to look at the remains. I got a call just now with the result. Positive. Reluctantly, the old bird indentified them. Her missing son Gerry. She didn't want to admit anything else, of course, like a family quarrel. She said it was a mystery to her how he got there, but she did let out that the brothers fought over a woman.'

'So you think Henley killed him in a quarrel? Killed them both? Killed Tipper because he knew.'

'I do indeed.'

Charmian was quiet for a moment, then she said: 'George, do we know exactly where the blood on the grass came from?'

'The little bitch Trix. She got hurt when Dick killed Foggerty. A glancing blow from a bullet that ricocheted. I don't think he saw how badly she was bleeding when he walked her home. Out of his head himself, I suspect. But he must have noticed later because he carried her home under his cape, that's when the blood and hairs got on it. And, of course, they both probably had Foggerty's blood on them too. There was a hell of a lot of it about. Dick went home, changed his clothes and then took the spaniel out for its walk, and the rest you know. A bloody business all round.'

Charmian looked down at his hands. She was waiting. She could see he was getting ready for something more.

'I don't know if you've heard,' he said with some hesitation.

'But those photographs . . . they had a bit of a fire in the office. Some fool dropped a lighted cigarette-end down on a desk and the fire spread to a stack of folders. The negatives were there.' He stopped talking.

Charmian thought about it for a moment. I'm being protected, damn it, by a consortium of my peers. She didn't now whether to be furious or relieved.

'What a shame,' she said eventually.

It was the nearest she got to saying thank you. And come to think of it, the nearest that would have been accepted.

Then she started to laugh. George Rewley let himself smile. There was another pause while Charmian's mind went back to what really mattered. She thought about the blood and what lay under the grass. She said:

'Do you think you'll get Henley for the murders?'

'I shall have a jolly good try,' said George Rewley with conviction.

The processes of the law rolled slowly forward. Eddie Dick came up in court, and bail being refused, was remanded in custody. An intensive study was made of the premises of his employment agency and of its records, turning up many interesting facts about his involvement with Jake Henley and the porn ring. Jake Henley himself was, for the moment, walking free. But a watch was being kept on him and he was known to be in Cheasey.

'Old Mrs Dick must be turning in her grave,' was Mrs Beadle's comment, passing judgement as the longest resident of Merrywick. 'I swear she didn't know anything of what was going on. Not that she was herself anyway for the last few years, poor old lady. Lost her wits, but nice with it, poor soul.' They had been roughly the same age, girls at school together, but Mrs Beadle was spryer and in possession of all her faculties.

Charmian started to prepare herself for her new position. The affair of the photographs was known about, of course, but no one had seen them. She could imagine what might be said in private, but her joke had gone the rounds and done her good. 'She was cool,' they were saying. 'You have to hand it to her, a woman like that you have to respect.'

Inside she was very, very angry but she would work through it.

The weeks rolled by.

The news filtered through to her that Eddie Dick's bitch had had her pups, so she telephoned the vet. She owed that animal something.

'Six nice little pups,' the vet said cheerfully. 'She's feeding them well and they're suckling strongly.'

'I'll pay any bills.'

'Thanks. Just give a donation to the fund.'

She would make it a good one. 'What about the pups? What will become of them?'

'I'll find them happy homes. You wouldn't like one?'

'No, thanks. I've got a dog, a share in one, anyway. What are they like?' Dolly might take one, or Annie. She and Jack were going on a course at a centre devoted to meditation and peace, which seemed a good idea for both of them. Or Kate might like a dog, except that she and George Rewley were talking of marriage, into which a dog might or might not fit. The difficult triangular relationship between Dolly, Kate and George seemed to have resolved itself.

The vet answered thoughtfully that they were ginger-and-white and looked like their mother. 'I don't know who Dad was, some sort of game dog, I suspect, but he must have had very short legs.'

Charmian looked down at Benjy, reclining happily at her feet. 'Oh Ben, you were not running forward to protect Winnie that day in Maid of Honour Row. Eddie Dick must have had Trixie with him and you ran after her to do a bit of courting.' Sucessfully, too, as it now seemed; those hormones he was taking had done a good job.

Within minutes, her telephone rang. It was George Rewley. He sounded excited.

'We've got Henley. A confession from a Cheasey man, one of the Rivers clan, who helped him bury the two bodies. Our London bones expert built up the face on the Tipper skull and put the red wig on it. Shocked the chap into telling all. Henley's been grabbed in Cheasey. We're taking him in, and we'll hang on to him this time, believe you me; the charge will be murder.'

Charmian put the receiver down. It was over at last.

The bones had ceased their dance.